MEET THE GIRL TAL

Sabrina Wells is petite, with curly auburn hair, sparkling hazel eyes, and a bubbly personality. Sabrina loves magazines, shopping, sleepovers, and most of all, she loves talking to her best friends.

Katie Campbell is a straight-A student and super athlete. With her blond hair, blue eyes, and matching clothes, she's everyone's idea of Little Miss Perfect. But Katie has a few surprises for everyone, including herself!

Randy Zak has just moved to Acorn Falls from New York City, and is she ever cool! With her radical spiked haircut and her hip New York clothes, Randy teaches everyone just how much fun it is to be different.

Allison Cloud is a Native American Indian. Allison's supersmart and really beautiful. But she has one major problem: She's thirteen years old, five foot seven, and still growing!

HOUSE PARTY

By L. E. Blair

GIRL TALK® series created by Western Publishing Company, Inc.

Western Publishing Company, Inc., Racine, Wisconsin 53404

 Library of Congress Catalog Card Number: 91-75777   ISBN: 0-307-22023-0

R MCMXCIII

Text by Crystal Johnson

Chapter One

"Jean-Paul, do you really think we could go away? What about the children? How can we get away from work?" I heard my mom ask her new husband, whose name is Jean-Paul Beauvais.

"*Ma chérie!* Why do you worry so about everything? But I guess that's why I love you," Jean-Paul said, laughing softly.

I got to the french door of the dining room and looked in just as Jean-Paul gave Mom a big hug. They were standing next to the huge mahogany dining room table, which was already set for dinner with our blue-and-white antique china plates.

Mom and Jean-Paul are still newlyweds, and they sure act like it. They're really goofy sometimes! I cleared my throat to let them know I was there before they started kissing or something.

"Oh, Katie!" Mom looked a little flustered

when she saw me.

"Hi, Mom. Hi, Jean-Paul," I said. My real father died three years ago, and I guess I'm not quite ready to call Jean-Paul "Dad" yet. But he's really nice to all of us, not to mention handsome.

"*Bonjour*, Katie," Jean-Paul greeted me with a smile. He's French-Canadian, so I hear a lot of French in our house now.

"Katie, can you please go tell Emily and Michel to come down to dinner?" Mom asked. She had called me downstairs early so that we could figure out a good time for the two of us to go shopping for new clothes for me. But she seemed to have forgotten all about that now. I guess whatever she and Jean-Paul were talking about was more important.

"Sure, I'll get them right away," I told Mom. As I headed back out of the room, I practically ran into our gardener, Mr. O'Reilly. Luckily, he stepped quickly to the side, so we avoided a major collision.

"Here you go, Mrs. B. Posies I picked myself, fresh from the hothouse," Mr. O'Reilly told Mom politely in his Irish brogue. "I thought you might be liking them for the dinner table."

He handed my mom a huge basket filled with flowers. They were really pretty, and they smelled great!

"Oh, Mr. O'Reilly, they're wonderful!" Mom exclaimed. "Thank you." She took the basket and placed it on the long, low mahogany sideboard that matched the dining room table. Then she picked one rose out and held it to her nose.

I thought Mom really looked beautiful, standing there with the rose. She has short, wavy blond hair and bright blue eyes. Jean-Paul says that my sister and I look just like Mom. I mean, we do all have the same color hair, but Mom has a body wave, while Emily and I both have straight hair. The three of us also have blue eyes. I never think of myself as being beautiful, though. I'm just . . . well, Katie.

"Oh, and I wanted to let you know that I'll be away next weekend," Mr. O'Reilly told Mom and Jean-Paul. "My daughter in Chicago just had a baby, and I'll be visiting her and the little one for a few days."

"Congratulations!" Mom and Jean-Paul both said.

Suddenly I realized I was just standing there eavesdropping instead of going to get Emily and Michel like my mom had asked. I started toward the back stairs, which are just off the kitchen, then hesitated again when I heard pots banging.

Cook must just be finishing dinner, I figured. Usually I try to avoid the kitchen when she's working. She's kind of grumpy, and I don't like to get in her way. Then I heard Michel's voice in there, too, so I decided to go in.

"Ah, Cook," Michel was saying, "this soufflé is *magnifique! Incroyable! Merveilleux!*"

Michel is Jean-Paul's son and my new brother. He's tall, with dark hair and nice brown eyes, and he's in the seventh grade with me at Bradley Junior High. We're on the hockey team together.

I couldn't believe my eyes when I walked into the kitchen. Michel was standing next to Cook with a spoon in his hand, and Cook was actually blushing from his French compliments! When she saw me, of course, she just glowered, so I decided to get out of there fast.

"Mom and Jean-Paul want us to sit down for dinner now," I told Michel. Then I ran up the back stairs to find my older sister, Emily, up in her bedroom on the fourth floor.

Pretty soon we were all sitting down at the dining room table. Cook came in with a large bowl of Caesar salad and began to spoon it out onto our salad plates.

Having dinner in our new house is kind of like eating in a restaurant and being waited on every night. It's really different from the way we used to eat. Sometimes Mom would leave meat loaf in the microwave for Emily and me if she had to work late at the bank.

In fact, everything is really different from the way we lived before Mom married Jean-Paul, who happens to be one of the richest men in Acorn Falls, Minnesota, where we live. I mean, besides Cook and Mr. O'Reilly, we even have a housekeeper named Mrs. Smith. That seems like a lot of people to take care of just the five of us, but I guess I'm getting used to it.

"So, Eileen, can we go?" Jean-Paul asked my mom after the salad had been served.

"I don't know. I'm still worried about the children," Mom said, giving Emily, Michel, and me a concerned look.

I didn't have a clue to what they were talking about. Apparently, neither did Michel and Emily.

"Go where?" Michel wanted to know.

"Why are you worried about us?" Emily asked. She didn't look very happy that Mom had called her a child.

Jean-Paul looked at Mom expectantly. "I would like to take your mother away for a few days, but —"

"Mother, I am sixteen years old," Emily interrupted. "That's old enough to take care of myself and Katie and Michel. I've been baby-sitting for other people since I was twelve!"

Mom didn't look convinced, though. "Emily, baby-sitting for a few hours is very different from being left alone for days while your parents are out of the country," she said.

"Out of the country!" I exclaimed. "Where are you going?" Mom and Jean-Paul had just gotten back from their honeymoon in France less than two months ago. Going someplace far away again so soon seemed pretty extreme.

Jean-Paul's dark eyes sparkled as he smiled at me. "It's only Bermuda, Katie," he said calmly. "Just a few hours away by plane."

Even though Jean-Paul was talking to me, I had the feeling he was trying to convince Mom, too. "We can leave Thursday and be home

Sunday. Besides, Mrs. Smith will be here until after dinner every day we're gone."

"But Mr. O'Reilly will be away, too," Mom said worriedly.

"Eileen, it's only for three nights. We have a state-of-the-art alarm system and very responsible children," Jean-Paul insisted. "Besides, how often can you and I get away from work at the same time?"

"Well, that's true," Mom said, but she still looked doubtful.

I glanced at Michel, who looked excited about the idea of being on our own for a whole long weekend. Next to him, Emily looked hurt and angry. "Mother, if you don't trust me to run this house . . ." Her voice trailed off into a furious huff.

Actually, I could understand Mom's point of view. After all, we had never been left alone overnight before, and our big new house still felt a little strange and scary at night.

"Emily is right, Eileen," Jean-Paul said. "She is perfectly capable of being in charge of the house when Mrs. Smith and Cook are not here."

Emily got a smug, satisfied look on her face. Suddenly I had a bad feeling that if Mom did decide Emily could be in charge, Emily would act like some kind of crazed army general or something. "Why should Emily get to be in charge, just because she's the oldest?" I asked. "I can take care of things just as well as she can."

"Me too," Michel chimed in.

"Thirteen is just too young," Mom said firmly. After a long pause she added, "But I guess it would be all right for Emily to take care of things while we're gone. I want to call the town police before we leave and tell them we'll be away so they can keep an eye on the house. And I'll see if Cook or Mrs. Smith can come in and make the children lunch on Sunday."

"Mom, I can cook for the children on Sunday," Emily said in her most mature voice. Then she smiled sweetly at Michel and me.

I looked suspiciously at her. Somehow, in the last few minutes, Emily had gone from being *one* of the children to being *in control* of the children. Suddenly I could see that living with Emily while Mom and Jean-Paul were away was going to be anything but fun!

Chapter Two

"Wow! I can't believe Mom and Dad will be away for three whole nights!" Michel said to me Friday morning as we walked out to the garage, where Emily was warming up her car. She drops us off at Bradley every morning before she goes to high school.

I shrugged. Actually, I didn't see what there was to be so excited about.

"It will be party time, eh, K.C.?" Michel added, calling me by the nickname all the guys on the hockey team use for me. *K.C.* stands for my name, Katie Campbell. He nudged me in the side with his elbow and smiled mischievously.

I stopped in my tracks and stared at him. "Are you crazy!" I cried. "We can't have a party. Mom and Jean-Paul are trusting us to be responsible while they're gone. Besides, Emily would never let us."

I looked quickly around to see if Emily had

9

overheard us. Her car windows were up, and her head was bobbing to the radio. I doubted she'd heard anything. When I turned back to Michel, he was looking at me in surprise. I guess he had expected me to go along with this party thing.

"Okay, chill out!" he said, shrugging his shoulders. "No party."

I almost started laughing at how funny Michel sounded saying "chill out" in his heavy French-Canadian accent, but I stopped myself. I didn't want him to think I wasn't serious about this. I guess I got my point across, because Michel didn't say anything else about partying during the drive to Bradley Junior High.

The ride to school is pretty interesting, since we go through almost every part of town. First we go past all the huge estates and beautiful houses in our neighborhood. As we get closer to the center of town, where Bradley is, the houses we pass are smaller and closer together. Then we drive by a gas station, Fitzie's Soda Shoppe, and all the small stores I used to walk past every day on my way to school when we lived in our old house.

My best friends, Sabrina Wells, Randy Zak,

and Allison Cloud, live in this part of town. I really miss living near them. I used to be able to walk over to their houses any time I wanted. Now I have to ask Emily, Mom, or Mrs. Smith for a ride. It's kind of a pain.

Soon we pulled up in front of Bradley. As Emily stopped the car, I saw Sabrina going into school. She has long, curly auburn hair that really stands out, so I knew it was her.

Saying good-bye to Emily, I hurried up the front steps and tried to catch up with Sabs. I didn't wait for Michel — he always runs off to find his friends, anyway.

I pushed through the crowd of students by the front door and headed for the locker that Sabs and I have shared since the beginning of the year. When I got there, Sabs was struggling to open the combination lock. She has a big battle with that lock just about every day, and usually the lock wins! Luckily for her, I usually get to our locker first and open it.

That's what my whole friendship with Sabs is like. We're really different, but we complement each other perfectly. I love the way she gets dramatic and excited about things. I'm a little more quiet and practical, but Sabs says that's

11

why I'm a good influence on her.

"Hi, Katie! I'm really glad you're here," Sabs said when she saw me coming down the hall. "I keep forgetting, do I spin left to fourteen, or right?"

"Right. Here, I'll do it," I offered. I spun the lock quickly, and it popped open with no problem.

"You're amazing!" Sabs said. She took off her fluffy down coat and hung it up. Then she began sifting through the mess of books on the bottom of the locker, looking for her math book for first period. Sabs found it, and then fixed the barrettes that were holding her hair off her face. She's kind of short, so she had to stand on tiptoes to see into the small mirror on the inside of our locker door.

I hung my purple down coat on the hook and emptied the books from my backpack, putting them in neat piles on the top shelf.

"*Hola! Qué pasa?*" Randy said as she and Allison walked up behind us.

Randy knows Spanish from when she lived in New York City before moving here last summer. I had picked up enough from listening to her to know that she had said hello and asked what's up. I answered, *"Nada,"* which means "nothing much."

"Very good, Katie!" Randy said, smiling at me. *"Molto bene."*

Sabs crinkled up her nose. "Hey, that's Italian, isn't it?" she asked. "Stop confusing us, Ran!"

"Sorry, Sabs. I have a quiz today," Randy explained.

Italian is Randy's first-period class. Whenever she has a test, she bombards us with weird phrases. Between her, Michel, and Jean-Paul, I was starting to feel like I was living at the United Nations instead of in Acorn Falls, Minnesota!

"I'll have to teach you guys a few Chippewa words, too," Allison put in, laughing softly. "Then you'll get really confused."

Oh, I forgot to include Al in my Acorn Falls United Nations before. She's one-hundred-percent Chippewa. Al told me that the Chippewa settled in Minnesota in the sixteenth century and that they still have a big Native American population around here, along with the Sioux.

"Cool!" said Sabs. "We can all learn."

I thought that would be a good idea, too. "Hey, how are your mom and the new baby doing?" I asked Al.

Allison's mom had a baby recently. I guess Al's getting used to it now, but it meant a lot of changes for everyone in her family. I could certainly relate to that, having a new brother, a new father, and a new house myself.

"They're doing great," Al told me. "I even think Barrett recognizes me now. She smiles all the time."

"She's probably just got gas," said Randy, laughing.

"Randy!" Sabs exclaimed, but she was giggling, too. It was kind of funny, but I hoped Al wasn't insulted.

"Oh, she knows I'm only teasing, right, Al?" Randy asked Allison.

Those two are pretty much opposites, too. Today they even looked opposite — Randy was wearing a black velour top with black stretchy pants, and Al had on a white sweater dress. They complement each other really well, though, just like Sabs and me. That's probably why they became such good friends.

"So listen, can everybody go to the mall and my house tomorrow?" Sabs asked, totally changing the subject. "You don't have to baby-sit, do you, Al?"

My friends and I go to the Widmere Mall a lot on the weekends to shop and see movies and stuff. We usually end up running into almost everyone we know from school there. It's really fun. I had totally forgotten that this Saturday Sabs wanted us to go back to her house afterward for a sleepover.

I love going over to Sabs's house. She has four brothers and a dog named Cinnamon, and there are always tons of friends there, too. Mr. and Mrs. Wells are really great about us coming over. They always say that with five kids running around already, what harm could a few more do!

"I'll be there," said Al. She used to get stuck baby-sitting her little brother a lot. Now, with the new baby, her parents hired a mother's helper so Al wouldn't feel tied down.

"Great! And you two can come, right?" Sabs asked, turning to Randy and me.

"No problemo!" Randy answered, pushing her spiky bangs out of her eyes.

"I forgot to ask Mom last night, but I'll ask today," I told Sabs. "She's having some kind of dinner party tomorrow night for people from the Acorn Falls Country Club. But I don't think kids are allowed, so I'm sure there won't be a problem."

"The Acorn Falls Country Club?" Sabs said, looking impressed. "Is Jean-Paul going to join?"

I shrugged. "I guess so."

"I bet that place is a real snob factory!" Randy joked.

Actually, I was a little afraid of that myself. I didn't really know any members of the country club, but I knew only the richest people in the county belonged.

Just then the warning bell for first class rang. "I can't wait for this day to be over so it will be the weekend!" Sabs groaned.

"I can't wait for my quiz to be over!" Randy added. "*Ciao*, you guys."

"Good luck, Randy," Al told her. "See you in homeroom, Katie." Then we were all rushing in different directions so we wouldn't be late.

The day flew by. Before I knew it, I was saying good-bye to my friends after school. Sabs made me promise to call her the minute I found out if I could come over the next day.

I called home and told Mrs. Smith I was ready to get picked up. Emily used to drive

Michel and me back and forth to school, but it got really complicated coordinating everyone's plans. So now Emily drives us to school and Mrs. Smith drives us home. Michel wasn't going home until later, so I waited alone inside the front door of school until Mrs. Smith's black car pulled up.

When we got home, I saw that Mom's red BMW was in the garage. She gets home early from the bank on Fridays. I figured this would be the perfect time to ask her about tomorrow.

"Mom?" I called as soon as I ran in the front door. I struggled to get my coat off and then hung it in the foyer coat closet.

It was amazing that Mom heard me from her second-floor office. "Hi, sweetie!" she called back.

I ran up the stairs, my knapsack in my hand, and opened the door to her office. It's a really pretty room, with lots of sunshine and over-stuffed flowered chairs and wicker baskets full of dried flowers. Mom was sitting behind her elegant wooden desk, making some kind of list. She was still wearing the blue suit she had worn to work.

"Oh, Katie, I'm so glad you're here," she

said, smiling at me. "I've gone through my closet, and I don't have anything appropriate for tomorrow's dinner party. As long as we were planning to do some clothes shopping, anyway, why don't we drive into Minneapolis tomorrow morning? We can be back in plenty of time for the dinner party, particularly since Mrs. Smith and Cook and the other people we hired to help out will have the food and details under control."

"Tomorrow! Mom, can't we do it next weekend or after school or something?" I cried.

Mom shook her head. "No, Katie, we can't. Jean-Paul and I are going to Bermuda this Thursday, remember? I need clothes for the trip, too," she explained.

"Why don't you just go shopping for you. I really don't need new clothes," I protested.

"Yes, you do, dear. What do you think you're going to wear tomorrow night to the dinner party?" Mom asked.

"Do I have to go? I thought it was just for adults," I said. This was getting worse every second. It looked like I would miss out on the mall and Sabs's sleepover.

"Well, it is for adults, honey. But I would like

the people from the country club to meet our children. What do you have to do tomorrow night that's so important?" Mom asked.

"We were going to go to Sabs's to watch videos and order pizza and sleep over," I explained. Suddenly it didn't sound like a very good reason.

Mom gave me a stern look. "Katie, you can do that anytime," she said patiently. "This is very important to me. I'm sure your friends will understand."

I lowered my eyes, feeling very selfish. "You're right, Mom. I'm sorry. But after I meet the country club people, then can.I go over to Sabs's?" I asked hopefully.

"We'll see, dear," Mom told me. "If it's not too late, maybe Emily will take you over."

I hate Mom's "we'll see's." They usually mean I don't have a chance of getting what I want. But I decided to keep my hopes up.

"Okay. I'll call Sabs now," I said quietly.

I sighed as I left the room. I had been really excited about spending tomorrow with my friends. Now it looked like my whole Saturday was going to be ruined.

Chapter Three

I woke up the next morning realizing that someone was knocking on my bedroom door.

"Katie, time to get up!" Mom's voice came softly from the door.

I managed to mumble, "Okay, Mom." My eyes focused, and finally I could see Mom's cheerful and very awake face peeking in my door. "What time is it?" I asked, rubbing my eyes.

"It's almost eight o'clock," Mom told me. "I want to leave here by nine so we can drive into Minneapolis and be there when the stores open at ten."

"Eight o'clock!" I groaned. On Saturdays I usually like to sleep late, at least until nine-thirty. I had stayed up late the night before reading a book, so I still felt tired. I had really gotten into the story and couldn't put it down until I finished it.

Mom smiled sympathetically. "Wake up, sleepyhead! I've got your favorite muffins and croissants warming in the oven so we can have something good to eat before the long drive into the city," she said. "Hurry and take your shower and meet me in the kitchen." Then she closed the door.

I sighed. Oh, well. I figured that as long as I had to go through with this shopping trip, I might as well make the best of it. Sabs hadn't been happy when I called her the night before and said that I couldn't go to the mall today. But she said she'd keep her fingers crossed that I could come over tonight after Mom's party.

I got out of bed and went into the bathroom that Michel and I share. One good thing about getting up this early was that I got to use the shower before he had a chance to mess everything up. I knew he wouldn't be awake for at least another hour.

A long hot shower made me feel awake, and I was starting to get hungry. I couldn't wait to have one of those fresh muffins Mom had picked up. I hoped she had gotten some blueberry ones. They're my favorite.

I quickly dried my hair and did it into a

French braid. Then I opened the door to my walk-in closet and looked at my clothes hanging in neat rows along the walls. There was a lot of empty space in there. Maybe I did need some new things to wear.

Walking over to the shelves where all my sweaters and sweatshirts were stacked, I picked out an electric-blue cotton cropped sweater that Sabs says matches my eyes perfectly. Then I chose a cream-colored pair of corduroys, a matching turtleneck, and some cream socks, and a blue scrunchy to wrap around the bottom of my French braid. Then I put on my loafers, and I was dressed.

I grabbed my watch out of my jewelry box and glanced at the time as I strapped it around my wrist. Eight-forty. Good, I was starving!

I trotted down the back stairs to the kitchen, two flights down. When I got there, Mom was standing at the stove, stirring something in a pot on the burner. It was almost like before she got married to Jean-Paul, when I would wake up every morning and come down to the kitchen to find Mom making breakfast for Emily and me. Except before, she was in our small yellow kitchen in our old house, and now she was in a huge kitchen with professional stainless-steel appliances and a black-and-white-tile floor.

"Oh, Katie! I didn't hear you come down. I'm just making you your favorite — home-made hot chocolate," Mom said brightly.

"Thanks, Mom. It smells great," I said, walking over to the cabinet to find us two mugs for the hot chocolate. The first door I opened only had plates behind it. I was still getting used to where everything is in our new house. I closed that door and then opened the one next to it. There were the mugs and glasses. Taking down two mugs, I set them on the counter next to the stove.

"I've got the muffins and croissants and fresh fruit set up in the dining room," Mom said. She grabbed a pot holder and carefully poured the steaming chocolate into the mugs.

I stopped and turned to Mom. "Um, do you think we could eat breakfast in here at the kitchen table? The dining room table is so . . . big."

Mom looked a little surprised, but then she gave me a warm smile. "Sure, honey. We'll be a lot cozier in here," she agreed.

She walked over to the round kitchen table and set down the mugs of hot chocolate, while I ran into the dining room. I grabbed the basket of muffins and fruit, along with the two plates and linen napkins Mom had put out for us, and brought everything into the kitchen. Then I sat down and picked out a beautifully browned blueberry muffin.

"Mom, how come Emily isn't coming shopping with us?" I asked. "Doesn't she need something to wear tonight, too?" I broke off a piece of the muffin and popped it into my mouth. It was delicious!

"She has a basketball game today. She is the captain of the pom-pom squad, so she really can't miss a game," Mom explained.

Every time she mentioned Emily's being the captain of the squad, I couldn't help thinking that Mom was disappointed that I had quit the flag team and joined the boys' hockey team. Still, I knew she was proud of me. I mean, we won the state championships, and I was even going to be captain of the team next year.

"Besides," Mom continued, breaking off a piece of croissant, "Emily has that nice sweater dress she wore to the rehearsal dinner before

24

the wedding. Remember? She's going to wear that. She and I decided that we'll spend a shopping day together when Jean-Paul and I return from Bermuda."

"Oh," I said. What else could I say? It still didn't seem fair that out of the three kids in this family, I was the only one who had to give up her Saturday to go shopping for something to wear for a party that I didn't even want to go to. But it was too late to do anything about it.

Mom glanced down at her watch. "We'd better get going. Finish up your hot chocolate, and I'll go grab my purse," she told me.

"Okay," I said softly.

Once I was in the car and we got closer to Minneapolis, I forgot how upset I was about not going to the mall with my friends. Minneapolis is totally different from Acorn Falls. The city is on the Mississippi River, and it really is beautiful and fun. There are so many people and stores there, and everything is so big. I don't think I'd want to live in a big city like Minneapolis or New York or anything. But it's fun to visit.

"I thought we could start at the big new indoor mall they just finished," Mom said, keeping her eyes on the road. "We'll go to that boutique I like and get a dress for me and maybe something for you, and then we could stop for some lunch. Would you like that?"

"Sure," I agreed. I wasn't sure what the difference was between a "boutique" and the regular old stores my friends and I usually went to.

We pulled into the huge parking lot of the mall and drove around until we finally found a spot. It was really crowded, considering that it was only a little after ten and the stores had been open for just a few minutes!

We parked and locked up the car and then walked for what seemed like a mile until we got to the entrance of the mall.

"Wow! Let's go in here!" I said excitedly, stopping in front of the biggest sporting goods store I had ever seen in my life.

Through the store's window I could see about a thousand hockey sticks lined up along one wall, and rows of skates. They even had those new roller blades, with the rollers in one straight line. Wearing those skates was supposed to feel the same as ice-skating, and I really wanted a pair. I thought it would be a great way to keep in shape for hockey season.

But Mom shook her head. "Not today, Katie. Let's just concentrate on new school and party clothes for you, and travel clothes for me. We'll come back another time for this." She smiled and walked toward the escalator.

I took one last look in the sporting goods store and then hurried to catch up with Mom. I definitely didn't want to lose her in the crowd of shoppers already pushing their way through the mall.

Mom led me upstairs and into a small store where classical music was playing. The place smelled like flowers. There was plush carpeting on the floor and rose-colored cushioned chairs to sit in. There was even a table with magazines on it and a coffee machine.

The moment we walked in, a saleswoman walked over to Mom. She was dressed in a pretty pink suit and wore a white carnation above her name tag, which read HOPE REED.

"Hello. My name is Hope," the saleswoman said, smiling sweetly. "May I offer you some coffee or a croissant?"

"Actually, I'd love a cup of coffee. It's been a long drive," Mom said, smiling back.

I frowned at the Styrofoam cup the woman

was filling with coffee. Didn't the people in this store know that Styrofoam was bad for the environment? I thought Mom might get mad if I said anything, though, so I kept quiet and just looked around.

There were five salesladies in the small store, and Mom and I were the only customers! I felt like they were watching every move I made. Feeling very conspicuous, I walked over to a rack of dresses. I figured the sooner we found something for Mom, the sooner we could leave.

I glanced at the price tag of a pretty blue dress that I thought would look nice with Mom's eyes. Suddenly I gasped and dropped the tag. The dress cost over one thousand dollars! I looked at Mom and then back at the price tag. I had to warn her about the prices in this store before it was too late!

Chapter Four

Mom and Hope Reed both turned to look at me. I just smiled and turned away, and they kept talking. Boy, did I feel foolish!

I went back to the dress to look at the ticket again, trying not to be too obvious. Maybe I had read it wrong and it was only one hundred dollars. I twisted my head around and focused on the figure on the price tag. Nope, I was right the first time.

I'd never touched a thousand-dollar dress before! I took another look. The dress didn't look particularly special. It was made of silk and had a few sequins on it, but there was really nothing so wonderful about it that it was worth that much.

I wandered around the store some more while Mom told Hope Reed what she was looking for. Everything in the store cost hundreds, if not thousands, of dollars! I was sure Mom didn't realize how expensive everything was here. I had to get her attention and warn her. Then we could politely leave and go to another store.

I walked over to Mom and waited for my chance to get her away from the saleswoman.

"Oh, and I'll need some dress clothes for my daughter, also," Mom was saying. "Do you carry anything in her size?"

I opened my eyes wide. I had to talk to her, and quick!

"Yes, we do." Hope Reed looked me up and down, sizing me up. "Let me go in the back and pull a few things from stock. I'm sure you'll love them. Feel free to take a seat or look around." Then she disappeared behind a curtained doorway.

Now was my chance. "Mom, did you look at the prices?" I whispered. "We'd better tell her we don't like anything and go!" I glanced at the other salesladies to make sure they hadn't heard me. They all smiled sweetly at me. I smiled back.

When I turned back to Mom, she was calmly studying the same blue dress I had looked at before. She didn't seem upset about this situation at all.

"Mom, come on!" I urged.

"Katie, it's all right," Mom said softly. "We don't have to leave. Jean-Paul told me to spend whatever I like. And we do need new clothes."

"But look at the prices!" I hissed.

Mom just gave me this soft, kind of secret smile. "Honey, we don't have to worry about that anymore," she told me. "I know it seems like a lot to pay, but you have to understand that these clothes are much better quality than less expensive clothes. The materials are better, the workmanship, the fit — everything."

She took the blue dress from its rack, carried it over to the area where the chairs were, and hung it on a hook there. "I think I like that one," she told me and then sat on one of the pink chairs.

I walked over and plopped down in the other chair, still in shock. Hope came back through the curtained doorway a second later, wheeling a brass rack in front of her with about twenty suits and dresses on it.

She picked up the first thing on the rack, a flowing white pantsuit. "Now, I think this would be nice for dinner in Bermuda, Mrs. Beauvais."

"Yes, it's perfect. I'll try it on," Mom agreed, nodding.

Hope placed the white suit on the back of the rack and went to the next item. It was a long black halter dress with no back and a plunging neckline. "This is just the thing for dancing or a show on your trip."

I turned to see my mother's reaction. This dress was just too — I don't know — sexy for Mom! But she just smiled and said, "I'll try that one, too. I think Jean-Paul would like it."

Then she actually giggled! I could feel myself turning bright red. Shopping with my mom was getting weirder every second. Now I was really wishing I was at the Widmere Mall with Sabs, Allison, and Randy!

Luckily, Mom didn't like the next couple of outfits that Hope showed her. I was especially glad she didn't like the inchworm-green flared pants with the orange jacket. I mean, if she was going to spend a lot of money, at least she was spending it on pretty stuff.

She picked out a few more things she wanted to try on, including the blue silk dress, and then it was my turn.

Hope had brought out two outfits for me to

see for tonight's dinner party. They were both really beautiful, and Mom insisted I try them on right away.

When I was alone in the curtained dressing room, I took a peek at the tag of the dark green wool skirt I was pulling on. I let out a sigh of relief. It wasn't as expensive as I thought it would be — only one hundred and twenty dollars.

Only one hundred and twenty dollars! What was I thinking? I never thought I'd be relieved to find that a skirt cost that much. But compared to everything else in this store, it seemed cheap. Mom was right about one thing — the wool skirt was nicer than anything I'd ever put on before. It was so soft that it didn't even make me itch like my wool skating sweaters did. It fit really nice, too. The waist wasn't too big or too small, and it didn't pucker up when I sat down.

Hope Reed had picked out a cream-colored silk shirt to go with it. The silk felt cool and smooth against my skin. I buttoned it up and tucked it into the skirt. I couldn't help glancing at the price tag. The blouse cost more than the skirt!

"Katie, how does it look? Come on out and

let us see!" Mom called from outside the dressing room.

I peeked out from behind the curtain and then walked all the way out into the store so that Mom and Hope could see. All the other salesladies were still watching us, too. It was totally embarrassing.

"That looks wonderful on her," Hope told my mother. "The hunter green looks great with her blond hair!"

My mother nodded her agreement. "That will do perfectly for tonight's dinner party. Now, if only I can find something that easily!"

I turned to go back into the changing room and put my own clothes back on.

"Katie, try on the other outfit, too!" Mom called out to me. "You can use some nice clothes!"

I happened to think that the clothes I already had at home were nice, but I did what Mom told me.

I was a little sorry to take off the wool skirt and silk shirt, they felt so nice. But I did, and then I reached for the other outfit — a red plaid jumper with a crisp white blouse underneath. The jumper had these suspenderlike straps, and it took me a minute to get them untwisted.

Finally I was dressed, and I looked at my reflection in the dressing room mirror. I really liked the way the outfit looked on me.

"That is adorable! We'll take it," Mom said as soon as I opened the curtain to show her. "You can wear it to school, too, Katie."

To school! I never thought in a million years that I would wear anything that cost so much to school. What if I spilled chocolate milk or pizza sauce on it? I would just die!

I opened my mouth to say something, but Mom was already being whisked away by Hope into a different dressing room with her outfits. I turned and closed the curtain behind me, then changed back into my own clothes. When I was finished dressing, one of the other salesladies was there in a second to carry the skirt, blouses, and jumper over to the counter for me.

I wasn't sure what to do, so I just sat on one of the chairs and waited for Mom to come out in her new outfits.

Trying all those clothes on took forever. I was dying to ask if I could go down to the sporting goods store until she was done, but I didn't want to bother her. Besides, she kept asking me what I thought of everything. I think she just wanted assurance that she really did look beautiful enough in the clothes to spend so much money on them!

Of course, Mom looked great in everything. In the end, she decided to get the white pantsuit and the black backless halter dress for Bermuda, and the blue silk dress for the dinner party. Then, after lots of thank-yous and smiles from the salespeople, we were off to a shoe store to get matching shoes for our new clothes.

I got a pair of dark green suede flats that were really soft. They matched both my new skirt and my new jumper. Mom got a pair of white sandals, some black heels, and blue pumps that matched the blue silk dress perfectly.

"Okay! Now that the hard shopping is done, we have a chance to do some fun shopping," Mom said as we left the shoe store. She immediately headed off for the other end of the mall.

Great! I thought the sporting goods store would be a good place to start, but Mom obviously had something different in mind. Before I knew it, we were headed into another store with classical music and more salespeople than customers.

It was going to be a long day, I realized with a sigh. My stomach grumbled, and I held my hand over it, hoping that no one else had heard. How embarrassing! I hoped Mom would let us eat after we were done in this store.

She went right up to the salesman and told him what she was looking for, then handed him a piece of paper with Michel's sizes written on it. Boys have it really easy. They never have to go shopping and try on stuff and deal with moms dragging them all over the place.

The man disappeared into the back room, and Mom began to look around. "What do you think of this, Katie?" she asked, holding up a deep green sweater with a horse on the front.

"It's really pretty!" I exclaimed. The sweater was a beautiful color. Besides, I happen to love horses.

Mom held it up to me, checking the size. "This will be good for school and for when you're outside skating or riding," she told me.

I nodded, feeling excited. I couldn't believe I was starting to get into this.

Mom went through the store like a whirlwind. When she was done, I had two new pairs of corduroy pants, one pair of new jeans, a pleated wool skirt, and several soft cotton button-down shirts that were going to have my initials embroidered on the pocket. I also got the horse sweater and a new wool coat with really cool Indian designs on it. I hadn't gotten this many new clothes ever, not even at Christmas!

Mom picked out some dress pants and some casual pants for Michel, along with some shirts for him and a sweater, too. She got a new brown suede skirt for herself. Then she bought a nice gray wool cardigan sweater for Jean-Paul. For Emily, she chose a leather purse with a matching wallet. Then she bought me a leather backpack for school.

Finally we were done. It was a good thing. If we'd had any more packages, we would never have been able to carry them all!

"Mom, could we eat before we go home? I'm starving!" I asked hopefully.

"Sure," she agreed. "I could use something to eat myself."

We went to the mezzanine level, overlooking the mall's ground floor, where there were tons of different places to eat. I was afraid Mom was going to drag me to some fancy French restaurant or something, but she let me choose. I picked out a hamburger place, which was okay with Mom, since they had a salad bar, too.

I don't know how we made it to the car with all those packages after lunch, but we did. And then we were on our way home.

I was kind of tired by the time we got back to Acorn Falls. Shopping and driving so far take a lot of energy! I was really looking forward to getting inside and putting everything down.

When I opened the front door, I just stood there in shock. There were people scurrying all over the house, all dressed in black pants, white tuxedo shirts, and bow ties.

"Where did all these people come from?" I asked my mother.

"Oh, honey, they're the caterers — the people I hired to help with tonight's party. They won't be with us permanently."

I was certainly glad to hear that! I turned as Mrs. Smith came out of the parlor.

"Oh, good afternoon, Miss Katie. You're

home," she said cheerfully. "Let me take these up to your bedroom."

It was a relief to see someone I recognized. I handed her a few bags and kept the rest. "I'll help you. Some of them go to Michel's and Mom's rooms, anyway," I told her, and we headed up the main stairs.

The next couple of hours were crazy, with strangers running all over the house. Before I knew it, Michel, Emily, Mom, Jean-Paul, and I were all dressed up and sitting in the parlor waiting for the first guests to arrive.

"Mom, after I meet everyone, can I go to Sabs's house?" I asked hopefully. I glanced at the grandfather clock in the corner. It was already after eight. I had missed the pizza, but maybe I could still make the videos.

"We'll see how late it is when we're finished, honey," Mom answered.

Another "we'll see." Things were definitely not looking good for me.

The doorbell rang, and Mrs. Smith went to answer it. The next thing I knew, I was being introduced to a bald man and his wife. For the next hour, people kept coming. I felt like I had a smile plastered permanently on my face from saying hello to everyone, even though I didn't remember anyone's name!

I was really relieved when Mrs. Smith finally announced that dinner was served.

"You two and Emily can go to the family room if you want now," Mom whispered to me and Michel while the guests all filed out of the parlor and into the dining room. "But I would like you to stay nearby until everyone leaves. I'll have Mrs. Smith bring you some food."

I looked at my watch. It was already after nine. By the time everyone left, it would be much too late to go to Sabs's house.

I was feeling really low as I went to the family room to use the phone and call Sabs. I had spent the entire day and night doing things I didn't want to. This was definitely not the kind of Saturday night *I* would have planned!

Chapter Five

I was still feeling kind of down when I woke up on Sunday morning. I hated missing out on Sabs's sleepover. Later I would definitely have to call and find out everything they did.

After my shower I put on my new horse sweater and jeans. It wasn't a school day, but I couldn't resist wearing them. I pulled on a pair of green socks that matched the sweater and then slipped on my loafers. When I looked at myself in the mirror, I had to admit I looked pretty great. I still sort of felt like I shouldn't have all these new and expensive things. But they made me feel special, too.

I was about to go downstairs for breakfast when the phone on my bedside table rang. It was Sabs.

"Katie, hi! Listen, you have to come over right away. Did you eat breakfast yet?"

"Hi, Sabs," I said. "No, I didn't eat yet.

Why? What's up?"

"I was just saying how it's too bad that you couldn't sleep over last night and Al said let's call and see if you can come have breakfast with us and so I am!" Sabs said without even stopping to take a breath. "We're making pancakes. Randy's mixing the batter now, so you'd better hurry!"

I could hear Randy and Allison calling out in the background that I'd better get over there or else. Hearing that made me feel really happy that they were my friends.

"I'll be right there!" I told Sabs.

"Oh, and Sam says to tell Michel to meet him and Nick and Jason at Billy's. They're going to shoot some hoops," Sabs went on. Sam is her twin brother, who happens to be friends with Michel.

"Okay. Bye." Hanging up the phone, I ran to Mom and Jean-Paul's room to ask if Michel and I could go to Sabrina's. Mom was just getting ready to come downstairs, and she said it was okay for us to go.

Then I ran to Michel's room and called out Sam's message and added that Mom said we could go. Then I went upstairs to ask Emily to drive me over to the Wellses'. She wasn't too happy about taking me, but she couldn't say no. Driving Michel and me places is one of her responsibilities now that she has her own car — especially when Mrs. Smith isn't around.

When I got to Sabs's house, I ran into the kitchen before I even took off my coat.

"Katie!" Sabs exclaimed as soon as she saw me. "That coat is the greatest!"

"Thanks." I smiled, looking down at my new Indian-print wool coat. "I got it yesterday."

"Look at you!" Randy said, glancing up after she flipped a pancake on the Wellses' stove. A pile of finished pancakes was on the counter next to her. They smelled really great.

Allison was putting a jar of maple syrup on the kitchen table. "Hi, Katie," she said as I took off my coat. "I love your new sweater."

"Are those new jeans, too?" Sabs asked. "You got all those new things yesterday?"

I nodded. "You guys should see the new indoor supermall in Minneapolis. It's huge!" I told my friends excitedly. "We have to go there sometime!"

"Definitely!" Sabs agreed.

I noticed that Al was wearing a pin that had

bright squiggles and geometric shapes on it. "That's really cool," I told her. "Did you get it yesterday?"

Allison nodded.

"And I got this really nice purple jumpsuit," Sabs added. "I can't wait to wear it."

While we ran around putting juice and milk and glasses and plates on the table, Sabs, Al, and Randy made me tell them about all the other stuff I had gotten with my mom.

"What did you do, buy out Minneapolis?" Randy joked. She put the plate of pancakes on the table, and we all started digging in.

"Mom tried, believe me!" I said. "You should see what she bought for herself. One dress cost over a thousand dollars!"

The minute I said that, I was sorry I did. It sounded kind of stupid, like I was bragging or something. I mean, I never wanted my friends to feel bad because I had more money than they did.

"A thousand!" Sabs cried, her mouth dropping open. "What did it look like?"

I felt really self-conscious talking about this. Suddenly I could think of a million better things to do with a thousand dollars than buy one dress. After I finished describing the blue silk dress, I just kept eating my pancakes, hoping my friends would talk about something else now.

"It sounds really pretty," Al said. "I bet it looks great on your mother."

"Besides, your mom had to have something nice to wear with all those country club people going over to your house," Sabs put in. "Think how she would feel if she was wearing something a lot less nice than they had on."

Randy nodded, taking a bite of pancake and chewing it. "Once M had to wear something like that when she and D went to the music video awards. It was the coolest." I used to think it was weird that Randy called her mother "M" and her father "D," but now it seems very natural.

"Your mom wore a dress like that? I don't believe it!" Sabs exclaimed. "You mean, with sequins and everything?"

"Yup," Randy replied.

I tried to imagine Randy's mother in that kind of dress, but I just couldn't. She seems a lot more down-to-earth than that. Randy's father produces music videos in New York

City, and it sounds like a pretty glamorous business. I just met him recently, and he seemed totally different from Randy's mom. I guess maybe that had something to do with why they got divorced not too long ago.

"Anyway, I'm just glad that the whole dinner is over," I said. I was really happy that my friends understood about the dress. They were definitely the best friends anyone could have in the world.

"Hello, Mrs. Smith?" I said into the telephone receiver. "Could you pick me up at Fitzie's today, at about four-thirty?"

It was after school Monday afternoon, and Sabs was waiting with me by the pay phone next to Bradley's entrance.

"Yes, Fitzie's Soda Shoppe," I told Mrs. Smith. "It's about two blocks from school on Maple Street. . . . Great. Thank you. Bye." I hung up the phone.

"So can you go?" Sabs asked.

I nodded. "Sure. I'd better find Michel and tell him we're getting picked up there later."

"Oh — I already told him," Sabs said. "I saw him at his locker and told him we were probably going to Fitzie's. He said he'd meet us there." She turned bright red, the way she always does when she talks about Michel. Those two sort of have a crush on each other, but they're pretty shy about it.

I grabbed my new leather knapsack off the floor as Al and Randy walked up, and we all went outside.

"Good idea about going to Fitzie's, Sabs," Randy said. "I really need a cheeseburger and some fries. M is killing me with bean sprouts and yogurt lately!"

Randy's mom is really into health food, and I could understand why Randy would want a change. It's kind of how I feel after having too much gourmet cooking.

"At least you have food in your house," Allison told Randy. "Since the baby was born, half of our refrigerator is full of baby milk!"

When we got to Fitzie's, it was already crowded with kids from Bradley. The best booth by the jukebox was taken by some eighth-grade guys. The one next to it was empty, though, so we hurried over and sat down.

I grabbed a menu and looked at it. I had

been to Fitzie's so many times that I knew the menu almost by heart, but I liked to look at it anyway. Sometimes they have good specials.

"This is going to be some wild party Saturday night," a strange guy's voice came from the booth next to the jukebox. "I heard that the house is huge!"

I wondered who the guy was talking about. I hadn't heard about any big party Saturday night. It was probably at some eighth grader's house.

"I don't know whether to order a banana split or a super peanut-brittle sundae," Sabs said, bringing my attention back to our own table.

"I'm definitely having a big greasy cheeseburger with french fries and a real soda, not diet," Randy declared.

Allison frowned, looking at the menu. "I'd like to have one of those frozen-yogurt sundaes, but they're huge," she said. "I don't think I can finish a whole one."

That sounded really good to me. "I'll split one with you, Al," I told her. "What flavors do you want?"

We decided to get vanilla and banana with

marshmallow and strawberry sauce and whipped cream. Just as the waitress finished taking our order, Sabrina's twin brother, Sam, appeared at our table. His friends Nick Robbins, Jason McKee, Arizonna Blake, and Billy Dixon were with him.

"Hi, you guys!" Sam said, sitting down next to Randy and Al. Billy squeezed in next to him, while Nick sat down next to Sabs and me. Sometimes I feel like all of us are kind of a group, even though my friends and I don't hang out with the guys all the time.

"Hey, dudes!" Arizonna said, pulling up a chair. No matter how cold it is outside, Arizonna always looks like he's just getting home from the beach or something. I guess that's because he used to live in California and he still has this really light, sun-bleached blond hair.

"Katie, I heard about your big bash this Saturday night," Nick said, leaning over Sabs to look at me. "Michel didn't say what time we should come over, though."

"What!" I cried, feeling totally shocked.

"Michel invited us over Saturday night while your parents are away," Sam explained.

"I can't wait to try out your indoor pool!" He pretended to do the backstroke and ended up hitting the waitress, who was coming over with our orders.

"Katie! You didn't tell us you were having a party!" Sabs exclaimed. She seemed kind of hurt, but also excited.

"Because we're not!" I said, feeling panicked. "We can't have a party in the new house. What if something gets broken? Besides, Emily is in charge while Mom and Jean-Paul are away. She'll never agree to a party!"

Arizonna reached over and took one of Randy's french fries. "Well, you should tell Michel that. He invited all of us already, plus the whole hockey team," he told me. "This could get really big. I know how things in California are. Kids have parties, and dudes come from every school in the county. We counted two hundred once at a beach party."

"Two hundred!" I gasped. "I have to find Michel!" I stood up, practically knocking Nick and Sabs out of the booth.

"Hey, relax! He's not even here yet!" Nick said, catching hold of the table so he wouldn't fall. "He stayed after school with Scottie to shoot some hoops in the gym."

"Oh." I sat down again and jabbed at the yogurt sundae with my spoon.

"Don't worry, Katie. It's only Monday. We have plenty of time to tell everybody the party is off," Al assured me.

Sabs nodded. "Yeah, he only invited a few of the guys, and half of them are here."

"I guess," I said with a sigh. I still wasn't feeling much better. There was no way I would until I had talked to Michel and made sure he knew the party was off.

I picked a little at the yogurt sundae, but I really didn't have an appetite. I never do when I'm worried about something.

Finally I heard Michel's voice say, "*Bonjour*." I looked up as he came over to our booth.

This time Nick and Sabs were ready. The minute they heard Michel's voice, they jumped up and let me out of the booth.

"Michel, I have to talk to you — now!" I said, facing him.

"Okay, what's up?" Michel asked. Then he spotted the half-eaten sundae sitting on the table between Al and where I had been.

"Mmm. Are you going to finish that?" he asked Al.

"Uh, no. Go ahead," Allison offered.

The next thing I knew, Michel was sitting down next to Sabs and Nick and digging into our yogurt sundae. He was acting like I hadn't even said anything! Al looked at me expectantly. I guess she could see the explosion that was building up inside me.

Planting my hands on my hips, I turned to Michel. "I have to talk to you about the party Saturday night," I said, trying to keep my voice down. I didn't want all of Fitzie's hearing about this party that we weren't even going to have!

"*Oui*. You guys are coming, right?" Michel asked my friends in between bites of sundae.

"Michel, we can't have a party!" I told him. "I thought you agreed!"

"But it's just our friends," he said, giving me this innocent look. "That's not really a party, eh?"

He was trying to convince me, but it wasn't working. What Arizonna had told me about that party in California where two hundred kids came really scared me. I had to talk Michel out of this.

"Katie, it's four-thirty. Isn't Mrs. Smith picking you up now?" Al reminded me, pointing at the big old-fashioned clock on Fitzie's wall.

"Thanks, Al." I pulled a few dollars out of my backpack and left it on the table for the check. "See you tomorrow, guys."

I glared at Michel, who was shoveling in the last scoop of sundae. I didn't want him to think I was letting him off the hook. We were definitely going to talk about this party some more.

I spun around toward the door — and that was when I bumped smack into a tall guy who had just stood up from the booth right next to ours. He had been carrying a stack of books that I accidentally knocked to the floor when I bumped into him.

He had the bluest eyes I had ever seen, and wavy brown hair that was short around the sides and then grew long in back. He definitely looked cute in his jeans and a blue corduroy shirt.

I had seen him around school, and I knew his name was Ted Ginley and that he was in eighth grade. But I had never talked to him before or been this close to him. Suddenly I started feeling nervous and sick to my stomach.

I wished I hadn't eaten that sundae.

"Oh — I'm really sorry," I excused myself, feeling like an absolute klutz and totally embarrassed. I bent to pick up the books, and Ted started to do the same. Our heads knocked together with a loud clunk.

We both grabbed our heads, and everyone in both of our booths started cracking up. Talk about humiliating!

Ted smiled at me, laughing a little. "It's all right, I've got them," he said, holding up a hand to keep me from knocking into him again.

While he was bent over his books, I stared for a second at his wavy brown hair. All of a sudden he looked up at me with his clear, deep blue eyes, and I could feel my cheeks burning. Ted Ginley had caught me staring at him!

I guess I just stood there looking dumb for a minute until Michel poked me in the back. "I thought we had to go," he said.

"Uh, right. I'm really sorry," I apologized to Ted one last time. Then I got out of there as fast as I could.

Great. I had just made a total fool of myself in front of the cutest guy in the eighth grade. I felt like I could never go back into Fitzie's again!

Chapter Six

For the rest of the afternoon, I couldn't stop thinking about what had happened at Fitzie's.

I was almost relieved that Mom kept Michel and me really busy. First we had to drag suitcases up from the basement for her and Jean-Paul to take on their trip. And then Mom kept following us around with lists of important phone numbers and things for us to remember while they were gone.

All that running around didn't make me feel any calmer, though. At dinner I kept dropping things, and I could hardly eat.

"Katie, is everything okay?" Jean-Paul asked when I accidentally sent my peas flying across the tablecloth for the second time.

My mother gave me a worried look. "I hope you're not getting sick," she said. "Maybe we should cancel the trip."

"I'm fine, Mom," I said quickly. "Really."

Actually, I was starting to wish they would cancel their trip, but I didn't want to be a baby about the whole thing.

After dinner I went upstairs to my room to do my homework. I started doing math problems, but I couldn't concentrate on them. I was totally horrified when I looked down and saw that I had said that if $3x + 7 = 28$, then $x =$ Ted Ginley!

I gasped and crumpled up the paper. I had to do something to calm down! I decided right then and there to at least go straighten things out with Michel about the party.

Jumping up from my desk, I ran into the bathroom and knocked on the door that led to Michel's room.

"*Entrez!*" he called out from the other side.

I opened the door and walked in. Even with Mrs. Smith straightening up his room every day, Michel still managed to mess it up. There were clothes scattered on the floor, and the bedspread was all rumpled. Michel was lying in the middle of his bed, a history book propped open on his stomach.

"What's up?" he asked, tossing the book on the floor and sitting up against his pillows.

I walked into the room, being careful not to step on Michel's new pants, which were lying in a heap in front of the bathroom door. I pulled his desk chair over to the bed and sat down on it.

"Michel, you can't have that party Saturday night," I began.

Michel held up his hands. "I told you, it's not a party. It's just a couple of our friends coming over," he insisted.

"A couple! You already invited the whole hockey team, plus Sam, Nick, Jason, Billy, Arizonna, Sabs, Randy, and Allison," I told him, counting everyone off on my fingers. "That's a lot more than a couple."

"So?"

I couldn't believe Michel was being so calm and cool about this. "So! Arizonna told me that in California, kids come from all over the place to crash parties. Once, two hundred people came!"

Michel just laughed and said, "Oh, K.C., don't be silly. Are there even two hundred kids in Acorn Falls?"

"This isn't funny!" I told him, crossing my arms over my chest. "Mom trusts us!"

Michel swung his legs over the side of the bed and sat up straight, looking at me. "Our friends would never do anything bad, I am sure of it," he said seriously. "Don't you trust them?"

"Of course I do," I told him, feeling sheepish. I did trust our friends. It just seemed like so many other things could go wrong. "Emily will never let you have a party," I said, changing tactics.

"That's the amazing part," Michel said with a mischievous smile. "I heard Emily talking to Reed on the phone. They are planning to go to a high school party Saturday night. She won't even be home, so she doesn't have to know!"

I shot Michel a skeptical look. "You really think she won't come home and notice that people have been here?" I asked.

"So what if she does? What can she do? By then it will be too late. The party will be over!" Michel said gleefully.

"She can tell Mom and Jean-Paul!" I pointed out.

"*Oui!* But if she does that, she'll have to admit that she went out to a party and left us in the house alone. I don't think she'll risk getting in trouble like that," Michel reasoned.

"But what about Cook and Mrs. Smith?" I asked.

Of course, Michel had an answer for that, too. "Cook is off this weekend," he told me. "Mrs. Smith is leaving after dinner Saturday night, and she's off on Sunday. Mom and Dad won't be home until late Sunday afternoon, so we'll have plenty of time to clean up any mess before they get home. They'll never even know anyone was here."

Obviously Michel had really thought about this. I had to admit that everything he said made sense. And he had invited only our friends, so there was no reason to think that anything would go wrong. Maybe there was nothing to worry about after all.

"Pssst! Katie!" Sabrina hissed at me from across the lunch table on Thursday.

"What?" I asked, looking at her. She seemed really excited about something.

"Don't look now, but Ted Ginley is staring at you!" Sabs whispered. She was trying not to look obvious, but it wasn't working.

I froze with my peanut-butter-and-jelly

sandwich halfway to my mouth. "What should I do? Can I look yet?" I whispered back.

"I don't know," Sabs answered. "I don't want to look that way, either!"

Randy stopped talking to Allison and turned toward Sabs and me. "What are you two whispering about?" she asked loudly.

"Shhh!" Sabs and I both said at the same time.

"It's Ted Ginley," I told Randy in a low voice before she caught the attention of the whole lunchroom.

Of course, Randy immediately turned to stare at the table of eighth-grade guys next to us. I hoped Ted didn't see her.

"You mean that guy you bumped into Monday afternoon at Fitzie's?" Allison asked, sneaking a peek at his table. "He's really cute."

"Don't look!" Sabs whispered. After Al and Randy turned back to our table, Sabs told them, "That's him. He's been staring at Katie all through lunch!"

I felt really self-conscious. "I'm sure he was just looking at someone else," I mumbled. I had no idea why Ted would be staring at me. I didn't even know him. If he was looking at me, he was probably just telling his friends what a klutz I was or something.

"Sabs, do you think he likes Katie?" Randy asked in a low voice.

My face started burning, and I got a queasy feeling in my stomach. "That's crazy. He definitely doesn't."

Sabs crunched off the end of a carrot stick and chewed it thoughtfully. "I bet he does," she said. "I mean, you should see the way he keeps looking at you, Katie!"

I tried not to look at Ted's table, but I couldn't resist. I glanced up — and found myself staring right into Ted's blue eyes. He smiled at me, but I quickly lowered my eyes and pretended I hadn't seen him.

"He is staring at you," Al said softly. "I saw it."

"Okay, so maybe he is, but I'm sure it's not because he likes me," I said. I stared down at my sandwich again, but I couldn't take a bite. I had definitely lost my appetite.

"Hi, Katie." A familiar boy's voice startled me. I looked up to see Scottie Silver standing next to our table.

Scottie was the captain of the hockey team

last season. We're really good friends on the ice, but I'm still kind of nervous around him otherwise. I guess it's because I kind of like him. It was a total surprise to see him right then. I hoped he hadn't heard us talking about Ted!

"Um, hi, Scottie," I said.

"I heard about the party Saturday night. The guys and I will be there," Scottie told me. I knew he meant the rest of the hockey team when he said "the guys." They were all really nice. It was looking like Michel was right that the party wouldn't be a problem.

"Great!" I told him.

Scottie kicked a little at the floor with the toe of his sneaker. "Well, I have to go. See you Saturday."

"Okay. Bye." I guess it was my day for turning red, because I could feel my cheeks burning again.

"This is wild!" Randy commented when Scottie had left. "Katie, what kind of soap did you use in your shower this morning? It's making all the guys at Bradley go crazy over you!"

My friends started cracking up. "Scottie and I are just friends," I protested, but then I started giggling, too. This whole thing was pretty ridiculous.

"Ohmygosh!" Sabrina whispered suddenly.

"What now?" I asked, looking up.

I was staring directly at Ted Ginley's button-down flannel shirt. My mouth fell open in surprise. I couldn't even say hi. My heart started to pound so hard that I was sure he heard it. Luckily, Ted talked first.

"Hi. You're Katie Campbell, right?" he asked me.

Somehow I managed to nod.

"Hi, Ted. I'm Sabrina Wells, and this is Randy Zak and Allison Cloud," Sabs introduced everyone. Luckily for me, even though Sabs gets totally tongue-tied when a cute guy talks to her, she's fine when one talks to me.

Ted nodded to Sabs, Randy, and Al and then looked back down at me. "So, do you want to go to Fitzie's with me after school?" he asked.

I couldn't believe it. Ted Ginley had just come right out and asked me out! My stomach was churning worse than ever. I didn't dare look at my friends. I knew if I did, I would totally lose it.

Finally I cleared my throat and said, "Um, I can't. My parents are going away on vacation, and they're leaving this afternoon. I have to go right home. Sorry."

I guess it was stupid to tell him my whole life story like that, but I didn't want him to think I said no because I didn't like him or anything.

"No problem, I understand," Ted told me. He seemed cool about it, even though I had just turned him down.

Ted turned to go, but then he stopped and turned back. "How about Saturday night?" he asked me. "I heard about this party. It's supposed to be really great."

My heart started to pound. "I don't think I can," I said to him. Saturday night was the night of Michel's party. I wanted to be there to make sure everything went okay. Besides, I wasn't sure I wanted to go to some party alone with Ted, especially since I didn't really know him and my parents would be away.

Ted flashed me a big smile. "Come on, it'll be fun," he said. "It's supposedly in this mansion over by the Acorn Falls Country Club. Some guy named Michael or Mitchell or something is having it."

Suddenly I felt horrified. He was talking about my house! Arizonna was right — kids we didn't even know were coming to this party!

"That's my house," I blurted out.

"Really? Cool!" said Ted. "Then I'll see you there." Before I had a chance to say anything else, he walked back to his friends.

I just sat there in shock. When I finally looked at my friends, Sabs, Randy, and Al were all watching me.

"Katie, what are you going to do?" Allison asked, shooting a worried look in Ted's direction.

"I don't know!" I cried.

"Well, the party isn't your only problem," Randy told me. "Scottie doesn't look too happy that Ted was over here talking to you."

"Oh, no! Really?" I asked.

Randy nodded. "Yeah," she said, leaning forward excitedly. She nodded her head to the right. "Check it out. He's over there."

Glancing over, I saw Scottie standing on the other side of the cafeteria. He was staring at me, frowning. When he saw me looking at him, he turned around and stormed out of the cafeteria.

"Randy's right," Al commented. "Scottie does seem kind of upset."

I let out a big sigh. "You guys, I can't worry about Scottie right now! I have enough to worry about with this party."

I knew I should never have let Michel talk me into the party. But it was already Thursday — I didn't have any idea how we could stop the party from happening now! Even if we called it off this second, there were probably tons of kids who had heard about it already and would show up Saturday night, anyway.

I had to find Michel and figure something out right away!

Chapter Seven

"Do you know how many people are coming with this Ted guy?" Michel asked me as we walked into our house after school on Thursday. I had just finished telling him about Ted's coming to the party here Saturday night.

"No, but he said it was going to be a big party," I told Michel. "I bet a bunch of eighth graders are going to crash," I said nervously.

Michel rolled his eyes at me. "Stop exaggerating, K.C. Ted is probably just coming alone. And besides him, the only people who are going to be here Saturday are the ones I invited — the hockey team, Sam and the guys, and your friends."

"My friends?" I repeated blankly.

"*Oui.* Sabs, Allison, and Randy," Michel said. He was looking at me like I was a nuthead for not knowing who my own friends were. "You did invite them over, didn't you?"

I shook my head. "Actually, I didn't. I was hoping you would cancel the party."

Michel frowned at me. "Well, you don't have to come, but the party is on," he insisted. "Now stop worrying!"

He turned to go upstairs, then stopped short as my mom appeared on the landing just above him. She was wearing her coat and carrying a small suitcase.

"Stop worrying about what?" Mom asked, looking from Michel to me.

My heart stopped. Luckily, Michel spoke up, so I didn't have to.

"*Rien, maman,*" he said quickly. "Katie is worried about you and my father taking the airplane, since she has heard about the Bermuda Triangle."

Mom laughed and came the rest of the way down the stairs. "Oh, Katie. Those Bermuda Triangle stories are just speculation. There's nothing to worry about," she said.

"I hope you're right, Mom," I said. But I wasn't talking about the Bermuda Triangle at all.

Just then there was a honk outside. "There's our limousine," Mom said, getting a little jumpy. "Jean-Paul!" she called upstairs.

Five minutes later Mom and Jean-Paul were loading their matching luggage into the long black limo that they had hired to take them to the Minneapolis–St. Paul International Airport.

Mom suddenly got all teary-eyed and grabbed Emily and Michel and me in a big hug. My face practically got smothered in her coat. "Good-bye, I'll miss you all!" she said.

"*Mon Dieu*, Eileen. It's only three days," Jean-Paul said warmly. Then he kissed us each on the cheek and ruffled Michel's hair. "*Au revoir*. Be good. No wild parties, eh?"

I glanced worriedly at Michel, but he just smiled and laughed. The minute the limo doors were closed, I whispered in Michel's ear, "Why did he say that? He must know!"

Michel checked to make sure Emily was on the other side of the limo and couldn't hear us. "Of course he doesn't know," he whispered back. "He was just making a joke, you know?"

"Are you sure?" I asked.

Michel nodded. "If he did know, don't you think he would have said more to us than just 'No wild parties, eh'?" Michel said, imitating his father's voice.

"I guess so," I said.

I stopped talking as Emily walked over to where we were standing. The limo started to pull away, and we all waved until it disappeared down the street.

"Okay, kids, time to go do your homework!" Emily ordered, turning to Michel and me.

"What?" I cried in disbelief. Michel stood there looking as shocked as I was.

"You heard me," Emily said firmly. "It's time to do your homework. And no television until you're done."

I glared at my sister. The limo was barely out of sight, and already Emily was acting like a tyrant!

"I've managed to get my homework done without you telling me to for the last seven years of school," I said. "I sure don't need you telling me to do it now!"

With that I stormed into the house and went up to my room. I plopped down on my bed and rolled over onto my back. Just seeing my pink-flowered wallpaper and all of my things made me feel a little better. This was definitely the nicest place I could think of being right now.

I felt like I wanted to stay in here forever.

That way I wouldn't have to face Emily or Mrs. Smith or Cook. I was afraid that if I talked to anyone, I would have to lie to them about Saturday night — and I was already feeling guilty enough. Besides, I'm not a very good liar, probably because I try not to do it.

I thought about it all through dinner and while I did my homework, but there didn't seem to be any way around it. The party was happening, and I just had to make the best of it.

Just as I was drifting off to sleep that night, it suddenly hit me. What if I could persuade Emily to stay home on Saturday night? Then Michel would have to cancel the party!

Why hadn't I thought of that before! Jumping out of bed, I put on my robe and slippers. It was already Thursday night. I had to get this plan in action right away!

I ran up the stairs to Emily's room on the fourth floor. It was just my luck that she was on the telephone. She was probably talking to Reed or one of her girlfriends. I tried to get her attention, but she put her hand over the mouthpiece and said, "Katie, would you mind giving me a little privacy?"

I went back to my room to wait. I lay back

on my bed to read, and the next thing I knew, I was waking up and my bedside clock read 2:36 A.M.! There was nothing to do now except go to sleep and wait until the morning to talk to Emily.

Friday morning I woke up in a total panic. I must have dozed off after turning off my alarm, and by the time Michel finally got me up, I only had twenty minutes to get ready for school!

Needless to say, I didn't have time to talk to Emily before we left. And Michel was with us in the car, so I couldn't say anything then, either. It was already Friday. The party was tomorrow, and now I wouldn't be able to talk to Emily until after school today!

"Hi, Katie," Sabs greeted me when I got to our locker. She had managed to get the lock open today, and was just dumping her bookbag inside. "What's the matter? You don't look so good."

"Thanks," I answered sarcastically. I hung my coat up and started getting my books together for my first class.

Sabs's hand flew to her mouth. "Oh — I'm sorry, Katie. That's not what I meant. You always look great. I just mean, you look sad or tired or something. Are you sure you're okay?"

"This party thing has me really worried," I admitted. "I mean, half the school knows about it! I'm going to try to talk to Emily today after school. It's my last chance to get this party canceled before tomorrow."

I noticed that Sabs looked a little disappointed. "So, if you can't get Michel to call off the party, what are you going to do?" she asked. "Are you going to be there?"

"I guess so," I replied, shrugging. "I'll have to be there to make sure nothing bad happens."

For a second Sabs stood there biting her lip and looking at me. Finally she said, "So I guess you don't want me to be there, too."

Then it hit me. She was upset because I hadn't asked her to come to the party!

"Oh, Sabs!" I gasped. "I'm sorry I didn't invite you. It's just that I was worried about everything and didn't want to get involved with it, you know. I guess I was hoping the party wouldn't happen, so I didn't invite anybody."

Sabs nodded. "Then you don't want me to come, huh?" she said again. She turned abrupt-

sure the party is on. If it is, then I'll tell the other guys to come on over."

I wondered how many "other guys" he was talking about. Ted seemed really determined to come to this party.

"You probably shouldn't even bother," I said quickly. "I doubt my sister will change her mind."

"Hey, it's no bother," Ted said, grinning at me. "I'll catch you tomorrow!" He looked at me really intensely for a second, and then he pushed through the front door and left.

It wasn't until I saw Emily's blue car drive up a few minutes later that I realized I was clutching my stomach. It was completely tied up in knots.

I took a couple of deep breaths to calm myself, then ran out the front door of the school and down the steps.

"Hi, Emily!" I said as I got into the front seat of the car.

"Hi," she said, looking at me suspiciously. "Why are you so happy?"

"Oh, no reason. I guess I'm just excited about the three of us being home together tomorrow night. It's not often that you, I, and

Michel stay home on Saturday night together. We can make popcorn and watch TV like we used to do when we were little!"

I flashed Emily a big smile. So far, my plan was going great.

Emily looked a little uncomfortable. "Katie, I'm going to tell you a secret, and you have to swear not to tell Mom or Jean-Paul," she began, turning to glance at me.

I tried to look like I didn't know what was coming. "Okay, I swear," I told her.

"Well, tomorrow night is one of the biggest parties of the year at school," Emily explained. "All the basketball players and the cheerleaders will be there. I just have to go!"

Uh-oh, I thought. I hadn't realized that she wanted to go that badly. It might not be so easy to convince her to stay home.

"But Mom would never want you to leave Michel and me alone in that big old house," I said. "What if something happens? What if a burglar breaks in? What if . . ." I searched my mind, trying to think of something really extreme. "What if the house burns down!"

Emily's face fell, and she bit her lip. "I know, I feel horrible not telling Mom about it. But it's so important to me." She shot me a guilty look, then added, "Besides, you and Michel aren't babies. You know what to do in an emergency. Mom has a list of all the emergency numbers by every phone, and I'll leave you the number where I'll be."

Emily pressed her lips firmly together as she watched the road ahead of her.

"I don't know, Em," I said, trying one last time to change her mind.

"Oh, come on, Katie!" she exclaimed irritably. "You'll be fine. I'll call and check up on you, and I promise I'll be home before eleven. Okay? Now stop worrying!"

I slumped back against the car seat. My plan had failed miserably.

The rest of the way home, I stared silently out the window. The party was on, and everyone at Bradley Junior High was going to be there. Including Ted Ginley. I had never felt so excited and bummed out at the same time.

Chapter Eight

I woke up Saturday morning pretty late, probably because I'd had a terrible time falling asleep the night before. I was just so worried about the party!

I showered and put on my favorite jeans and a Bradley sweatshirt that Mom usually doesn't like me to wear because it's kind of worn out and faded. Then I dried my hair, put it back with a blue headband, and went down to the kitchen for breakfast.

Mrs. Smith was coming later to make us lunch and dinner and do some laundry, but she hadn't arrived yet. Emily and Michel were still upstairs, so I was all alone.

I could feel myself getting nervous while I ate my cereal. One thing was for sure — I knew that if I didn't keep very busy all day, I would go crazy!

Luckily, I had some library books that were

due. Instead of waiting and asking Emily or Mrs. Smith to take me there, I decided to ride my bike downtown. It was kind of far away, but it felt good to pedal around in the cold air.

By the time I got back home again, Mrs. Smith was there. Michel was up, too. We were both acting sort of edgy. It was kind of like we were both waiting for something. When I thought about it, I realized that Michel was waiting for the party to start, while I was waiting for it to end!

I had so much nervous energy that I finally went downstairs and ran a mile on the treadmill in the workout room. Then I swam fifty laps in our indoor pool. After that I was so exhausted that I didn't have any more energy left to worry.

I took another nice hot shower to soothe my tired muscles. Afterward I stood in my room in my terrycloth bathrobe, wondering what I should wear to the party. Sabs had told me she was going to call, but it was getting late and she hadn't yet. Maybe I would call her.

Just then my phone rang, and I jumped at the sound. It's kind of spooky when you wish for something to happen and then it does!

Grabbing the phone on my bedside table, I flopped down on my bed and said, "Sabs!"

"Katie? It's Mom!" Mom's voice was a little fuzzy, kind of like how Jean-Paul sounds when he calls us on his car phone.

"Mom! Where are you?" I said, sitting up straight. A terrible thought struck me. What if she and Jean-Paul decided to come back early and were calling from a limo on their way home? There was no way we could get in touch with everyone before the party and tell them not to come. It was already too late!

"We're in Bermuda, Katie. Where else would we be?" Mom said. I heard her chuckling into the phone. I hoped I hadn't gotten her suspicious.

"I just wanted to say hello and see if everything is all right," Mom went on. "How is everyone?"

"Fine. How's the weather there?" I asked. I really wanted to steer the conversation away from what was going on here.

"Beautiful! Warm and sunny. Oh, and the Bermuda Triangle was peaceful and calm, so don't worry," Mom said.

I rolled my eyes. I would never live down

that lie Michel had told. Now Mom thought I was silly enough to believe all the stories about the Bermuda Triangle. "That's good, Mom," I told her. "I won't worry. What time will you be home tomorrow?"

"It's all written down next to the phone in the kitchen. Didn't you see my note?" Mom asked. She was starting to sound worried that her note might be missing or something. The truth was, I hadn't bothered to read the note, since it was more like a mini-novel — five pages long, with writing on both sides of the paper!

"Well, never mind," Mom went on. "We'll be landing at about two o'clock. By the time we get our luggage, and if the limo doesn't hit too much traffic on the way home, we should be there by four."

"Okay, great! I'll see you then. Have fun. Love you!" I said, trying to get off the phone. I knew Mom would talk forever if she started to get sentimental and miss us. And anyway, this call had to be costing a fortune already.

"Okay, good-bye. See you tomorrow. Kiss Emily and Michel for me, and say hello to Mrs. Smith," Mom said.

"I will. Good-bye."

"Good-bye, Katie," Mom said. Then she finally hung up the phone.

I hung up my end, too. The phone rang again, almost immediately. What did Mom forget to tell me now?

"Hello?" I answered.

"Katie! It's Sabs."

I breathed a sigh of relief. "Hi, Sabs. What took you so long to call?" I asked.

I heard Sabs groan on the other end of the line. "Mom decided to have a family cleanup day, so I've been stuck in the garage sorting through tools and garbage for hours," she explained. "I'm filthy! Anyway, I just wanted to tell you that Randy, Al, and I will be over as soon as we eat dinner and Luke gets home from work to drive me. It'll probably be about seven."

That sounded perfect. Mrs. Smith would be leaving at about six-thirty, after she straightened up the kitchen after dinner.

"Great!" I told Sabs. "I'm so nervous —" I broke off as someone knocked on my door.

"I have to go, Sabs. Listen, I have no idea what's going to happen tonight, so come as soon as you can!" I said quickly. "Bye."

I hung up the phone, then called out, "Come in!"

My bedroom door opened, and Mrs. Smith popped her head in. "Miss Emily and Master Michel have both requested that dinner be served early tonight. Is that all right with you, Miss Katie?" the housekeeper asked me.

I kind of wished she would drop the "Miss" and "Master" stuff, but she always insisted on it. "That's fine," I said.

"Dinner will be served at five-thirty, then," said Mrs. Smith. With a slight nod, she closed my door softly.

I knew exactly why Emily and Michel had requested an early dinner. Emily wanted to eat and get ready for Reed to pick her up for her party at six-thirty. And Michel wanted Mrs. Smith out of here before any kids showed up for his party. I hoped he had told everyone not to come until at least seven o'clock. Early birds would ruin everything if Mrs. Smith saw them!

Dinner went by in a nerve-racking blur. Emily and Michel both finished eating in about two seconds flat. When they were done, Emily quickly ran up to her room and Michel went into the family room and turned on the television.

I looked at my watch and saw that it was only six o'clock. There was still plenty of time before people would be coming. I looked down at the jeans and sweatshirt I had thrown back on so that I wouldn't be late for dinner. I definitely didn't want to wear these to the party. I mean, even if the party was Michel's idea and I was against it, I didn't want to look like a slob.

I ran upstairs to my room and looked in my closet. First I picked out a pair of white corduroys and a pink button-down shirt. But then, as I reached up to get the shirt from its hanger, my hand brushed against the cream-colored pleated skirt I had gotten in Minneapolis. As soon as I felt the soft wool, I immediately changed my mind about what to wear.

Five minutes later I had on the skirt plus the cream-colored blouse Mom had gotten for me. It had gold braiding on the front, and it looked really nice with the skirt. Wearing my nice things made me feel a lot better about this whole party thing.

Michel gave me a funny look when I walked into the family room. "Nice outfit, K.C.," he told me. "So I guess you're not too upset about the party, after all."

"I just hope nothing goes wrong," I said.

Just then the grandfather clock in the parlor struck the half hour. It was six-thirty. Michel got an anxious look on his face. "Why isn't Mrs. Smith gone yet!" he whispered.

"You know how she is. She won't leave until everything is spotless," I reminded him. I tried to look calm, even though I was starting to get really nervous, too.

We both jumped when the front doorbell rang a second later. Michel flew out of his seat and headed for the foyer, with me right behind him. "I'll get it, Mrs. Smith!" he called over his shoulder. I had never seen him move that fast, not even on the ice during hockey games.

Michel slid to a stop in front of the door, opened it a few inches, and looked out. I looked around his shoulder and could see Sam's freckled face peering in at us.

"What's up?" Sam asked. Arizonna, Nick, Jason, and Billy were standing behind him.

"You're too early," Michel whispered out through the narrow opening. "Hide!"

I heard Emily come crashing down the stairs

behind us from her room on the fourth floor. She must have been afraid that Reed was here to pick her up, and she didn't want Mrs. Smith to see him. I looked up as she ran down the last flight with her hair flying straight out behind her.

Michel quickly slammed the door right in the surprised faces of the guys. Then Mrs. Smith came walking out of the kitchen. She had her coat and hat and gloves on, and she was heading right for the front door!

"That was just a salesman," Michel burst out. "I said we didn't want to buy anything and sent him away."

If I hadn't been so worried, I would have thought that this whole thing was hysterical. It was like we were in one of those Pink Panther movies or something, where everything that happens is totally ridiculous.

Mrs. Smith said good night and then opened the door. I held my breath as I looked out. I didn't know where the guys had gone, but right now they were nowhere in sight.

I let out my breath in a rush of relief. Michel looked relieved, too. Now all we had to do was wait until Emily left. I hoped it wouldn't be too long. It was really cold out. The guys were probably freezing.

The minute the door closed, Emily turned to me and said, "I was hoping Mrs. Smith would leave early, since we ate early. Reed should be here any minute. I almost died when the door-bell rang. Good thing it was the salesman, huh?" she said with a nervous laugh.

"Yes, it's a good thing," Michel repeated, looking at me.

We waited in the foyer with Emily for Reed to come. It seemed like forever before we heard him honk outside, but when I checked my watch, I saw that only four minutes had gone by.

"Bye!" said Emily. She grabbed her coat out of the closet and ran out to the car. Michel and I followed her onto the front steps. We waved and stood there out in the freezing cold watch-ing Reed's car drive away.

"*Mon Dieu!* That was a close one," Michel said after the car was out of sight.

"Definitely," I agreed, looking around the driveway and toward the garage. "We have to find the guys," I added. "It's cold out here!"

Suddenly the bushes next to the front door

started to shake, and then Sam, Arizonna, Billy, Jason, and Nick poked their heads out.

"Ohmygosh! How did you guys all fit in there!" I cried, laughing at the pieces of evergreen sticking in their hair and jackets.

Arizonna clambered up onto the steps and ran for the door, rubbing his arms. "Let me inside," he said through chattering teeth. "My California blood isn't made for Minnesota nights!"

"I've never been that close to nature before," Billy joked, walking behind Arizonna.

"We had to jump in there and hide when the door opened," Nick explained. He punched Michel lightly on the arm. "You sure throw an exciting party!"

"And this is only the beginning!" Sam added. "Come on, Jason." Sam grabbed Jason's hand to help him out of the bushes, where he was still standing looking dazed.

Michel and I followed everyone into the house and closed the door. The guys all stood in front of the big radiator in the foyer to warm up.

"I'm going into the kitchen and see if there are any chips or pretzels to eat," Michel said.

Earlier in the week I had heard him ask Cook to pick up some snacks at the supermarket. Usually we just have healthy stuff around, but since Cook and Michel seem to be such good friends lately, he gets whatever he wants.

"Great!" said Sam, his face lighting up.

"What are you guys doing here so early?" I asked, putting my hands on my hips. I was still shaking from the close call with Emily and Mrs. Smith. "Sabs said she was waiting for Luke to get home to drive her, and they wouldn't be here until seven."

Sam shrugged. "We didn't feel like waiting and then getting crushed in the back of the station wagon, so we walked over."

"But it's so far!" I cried. "It must have taken you half an hour."

"Yeah!" said Arizonna. His face was still red from the cold, but he had at least stopped shivering.

The front doorbell rang again, so I walked over and opened the door. Scottie Silver was standing there with Flip, Brian, and Peter from the hockey team.

"Hi, you guys," I said as they came in.

Our foyer is pretty big, but it was beginning

to fill up, so I decided to move everybody into the family room. That's where the stereo and pool table are. Mostly I just wanted to make sure no one went into the parlor or the dining room. That was where most of our antiques were, and I definitely did not want them to get broken.

Michel appeared in the family room right after we all moved in there. He had some bags of snacks in one hand, and cans of soda in the other. He put them all on the table in front of the couch. Flip immediately started searching through the CDs, and Scottie and Brian challenged Sam and Nick to a pool game.

I stood there and looked around. Things seemed to be going fine so far. Maybe I had been silly to worry. I glanced at my watch and saw that it was almost seven o'clock. I hoped that Sabs, Randy, and Allison would get here soon. So far I was the only girl here!

The doorbell rang again, and I ran out to the foyer to get it. I wondered who it would be this time.

"Hey, Katie," Ted said, grinning at me. "Glad to see the party's on!"

"Hi," I managed to say, trying not to stare at

Ted. A bunch of other eighth-grade guys were with him. I didn't want to act like a jerk with them watching.

Ted pushed past me, and his friends followed him in. Some of them were carrying brown paper grocery bags. Before I could even close the door, about twenty more people came in all at once. I didn't recognize most of them. I think some of the kids were even in high school!

I just stood there with my mouth open until I realized that people were starting to wander all over the house. Some headed toward the kitchen, a few more were wandering back to the family room, and some more were looking in all the doorways on the first floor. Things were definitely starting to get out of control!

Running into the family room, I grabbed Michel. "You have to do something!" I cried.

"K.C., there are a lot of people here I don't know," Michel said, looking around in confusion. He seemed to just be noticing all the strangers for the first time.

Just then the family room door flew open and Ted walked in. He was holding a beer bottle in one hand and a bottle of Jean-Paul's French cognac in the other hand.

"Hey, my dad has this stuff," Ted said, holding up the cognac. "It's really expensive." He walked right over to the stereo and cranked up the volume until the pictures on the walls began to shake.

Michel ran forward and grabbed the bottle of cognac out of Ted's hand. "My father will kill me if we have any of this!" he said. "And besides, there's no drinking here. It's not that kind of party."

Ted rolled his eyes at Michel and went right on drinking from his beer bottle. I couldn't believe he was being such a jerk. I mean, he had always seemed nice before.

Michel looked really nervous when he came back over to me. "I'm going to hide this somewhere!" he said.

As Michel ran out of the room, I clapped my hands over my ears. The music was deafening! I turned to lower the volume on the stereo, but I noticed that Scottie was already there. It looked like he and Ted were arguing.

Seeing them together made me feel really weird. I definitely did not want to go over there right now.

Looking around, I saw that a kid I didn't

even know was on the phone. Another was tossing CDs on the floor as he looked through our collection. Someone else was dancing on the pool table! A bowl of chips had been dumped on the floor, and they were already crushed into little pieces in the rug.

This was awful! I couldn't imagine what a disaster it would be if people got into the china cabinet in the dining room, or spilled soda on the parlor's handmade wool carpets!

"You jerk! Why don't you leave!" I heard Scottie's angry voice yelling above the music.

I whirled around and saw that Scottie and Ted were facing each other. Scottie was holding a pool stick in his hand and waving it at Ted. Ted looked like he was going to hit Scottie with his beer bottle.

"It's not your house!" Ted shouted back. "Katie invited me!"

I turned and screamed for Michel, but he wasn't anywhere around. The rest of the hockey team started to crowd around behind Scottie. And Ted's friends looked like they were just waiting for a fight to start so they could jump in. Sam, Nick, Jason, and Arizonna were by the pool table, looking totally shocked.

"Katie! Is there another phone?" Billy asked, suddenly appearing next to me. "I'm going to call my brothers and get them over here. This is totally out of hand!"

"Good idea!" I told him. Billy's brothers were older than him. I was sure they would be able to calm things down here.

Grabbing Billy's arm, I practically dragged him through the library to Jean-Paul's office to use the private line in there. I really wished my friends would get here. I needed all the help I could get!

Right after I showed Billy the phone, I heard the doorbell ring again. Maybe it was Sabs with Luke! I ran for the front door and flung it open.

My mouth fell open. The two people standing in front of me were definitely not Sabs and Luke. They were Acorn Falls police officers!

Chapter Nine

Randy calls Sabrina.

SABRINA: Hello!

RANDY: Sabs, it's already seven o'clock. What's the deal?

SABRINA: *(Sighing)* I know. I'm sorry, Ran. Luke isn't home from work yet. He must be working overtime or something. I was hoping that it was him when the phone rang.

RANDY: Well, M is home and she's taking a dinner break from her painting, so I can get her to drive us.

SABRINA: That would be great! Thanks, Randy.

RANDY: No prob. I'll get Al first, and then we'll swing by to get you. See you in a few.

SABRINA: Okay. Bye.

RANDY: *Ciao.*

Emily calls Sabrina.

SABRINA: Hello, Luke?

EMILY: Sabrina? It's not Luke. This is Emily. Is my sister there?

SABRINA: No, why? Where are you?

EMILY: At the high school basketball party. I've been calling home for twenty minutes now and the phone has been busy, so I called the operator. She said it's off the hook, so I tried Katie and Michel's line and there's no answer. *(There is a pause.)* I'm worried. I'm afraid something's wrong.

SABRINA: *(Silence.)*

EMILY: Sabrina?

SABRINA: Um, Emily, there's something I think you should know. Katie is probably going to kill me, but you're right, there could be something wrong.

EMILY: What are you talking about? What's going on?

SABRINA: Well, Michel planned this party for tonight.

EMILY: What!

SABRINA: It was supposed to be really small, just a few of the guys. But then a lot of people heard about it at school, even some guys in the eighth grade. Katie was really worried about it getting out of hand, but she didn't want to tell on Michel. We were supposed to be there to help her make sure everything is okay, but Luke is late.

EMILY: Thanks for telling me, Sabs. I'll have Reed drive me right over there.

SABRINA: I hope everything is all right.

EMILY: So do I. Good-bye.

SABRINA: Bye.

Sabrina calls Katie.
(Busy signal.)

Sabrina calls Allison.

ALLISON: Hello.

SABRINA: Hi, Al, it's Sabs. Is Randy there yet?

ALLISON: No, not yet. She should be here

any minute, though. Why?

SABRINA: You guys have to get over here right away so we can help Katie! I think there's something really wrong over at her house. Emily just called me and said the phone has been off the hook all night and no one answers on the other line. I got worried, so I told her about the party.

ALLISON: You did? Did she get mad?

SABRINA: I think she was too worried to be mad. She's going home right now.

ALLISON: I hope nothing terrible has happened.

SABRINA: Me too. I tried to call, but I got a busy signal, too. Sam and the other guys all went over early, though, so at least Katie and Michel will have some help.

ALLISON: Oh, Randy's car just pulled up. We'll be right there, Sabs! Goodbye.

SABRINA: Bye. I'll be waiting outside. Hurry!

Chapter Ten

Michel ran up behind me. When he saw the police officers, he stopped short. *"Mon Dieu!"* he said under his breath.

"Good evening," the first officer said, nodding his square, serious face. "Do you two live here?" His badge read TARKINTON.

"Yes, we do," I answered quickly. I tried to act casual, even though I was feeling more panicked than ever. Our house was a madhouse, and teenagers were even drinking beer! I didn't know much about the law, but it seemed like these police officers would have to arrest us.

"Your parents are away for the weekend, aren't they?" the second officer asked us. The name on his badge was HANNIGAN. "Mrs. Beauvais asked us to keep an eye on the house while they were gone."

I had totally forgotten Mom's mentioning that she was going to do that. Now I felt really ashamed and stupid for letting Michel have this party.

Michel looked pretty sheepish, too. "Yes, they're away," he said, looking down at the floor as he answered the officer's question.

We all turned at the sound of a loud crash coming from the family room, followed by some yelling.

"I'm sorry we had the party, Officers, but you have to hurry!" I said, speaking as fast as I could. I grabbed Officer Tarkinton's sleeve and pulled him toward the family room.

The next few minutes passed in a whirl-wind. The minute Ted and his friends saw the policemen, they stopped fighting and tried to run out the door. The policemen grabbed them and made them all sit down. Pretty soon everyone was sitting quietly. All those teenagers took up every inch of our family room!

One officer got everyone's names, while the other went around collecting the bottles of beer that were left. Michel and I just stood quietly near the family room door. I was shaking like a leaf, but at least everything had calmed down. Or at least that's what I thought until

Emily and Reed came in.

Emily looked like she was in total shock — especially when she saw the policemen.

Officer Tarkinton stopped writing down names and stared at Emily. "Now, who are you?" he asked.

"I'm Emily Campbell. I'm in charge while my parents are away," Emily told him. She looked really nervous.

Officer Tarkinton gave Emily a stern look. "Well, miss, it doesn't look like you're doing a very good job, does it?" he reprimanded her.

He took Emily and Reed out into the hall to talk while Officer Hannigan stayed in the family room and finished taking everyone's names.

"Ohmygosh!" Sabrina appeared right behind me in the family room doorway, wearing her new purple jumpsuit. Al and Randy were with her.

"Boy, am I glad you guys are here!" I told them. "This place was a madhouse!"

"Katie, I'm really sorry I told Emily about the party," said Sabs, "but she said the phone was off the hook, and we were all worried that something bad happened."

I turned to look at the family room phone, which I had seen one of Ted's friends using before. Sure enough, it was off the hook. I went to hang it back in its cradle and then went back to my friends.

"You definitely did the right thing, Sabs," I said. "If the police hadn't come, our house would have been totally destroyed!"

"You mean, worse than it is?" Randy asked, looking around.

The damage was pretty bad, I realized. The pool table was turned on its side. I figured that must have been the crash we had heard before. There were broken beer bottles all over, and a picture had fallen off the wall. Chips and pretzels were scattered over the floor, mixed with CDs and videotapes.

"It's a good thing we came over, Katie," Sabs said. "You're going to need a lot of help cleaning this place up before your mom and Jean-Paul get back tomorrow."

Al tugged thoughtfully on her braid as she looked around. "It's a good thing the police came when they did, too," she commented.

"That's for sure," I agreed.

A minute later Officer Tarkinton came back

into the family room, followed by Emily and Reed. The officer swept the room with his serious eyes. I noticed that all of the kids looked really afraid. They were probably imagining what their parents would say when these policemen called them up.

"I've decided not to press any charges against you kids, even though you are all minors and beer was found on the premises," Officer Tarkinton began.

I could hear everyone breathe a sigh of relief.

"However," he went on, "all of your names will be kept on file. If any of you get caught doing anything illegal again, we won't be so easy on you."

"And we are confiscating the beer," the other officer added, tapping the bag that held the bottles he had collected.

"Are you going to tell our parents?" Michel asked softly. He was standing right next to me, his hands stuffed into the pockets of his pants.

The two officers looked at each other for a second and then looked back at Michel and me. "I'll leave that decision up to you and your sister," Officer Tarkinton finally said. "She explained how you invited only a few friends over and then these others came. I think you've all learned your lesson. You should never have anyone over without your parents' permission and proper adult supervision."

"Yes, sir," Michel and I both said together.

"Okay, everybody out!" Officer Hannigan ordered, clapping his hands.

Everyone jumped up and got out of our house as fast as they could. Soon Sabs, Randy, Al, Sam, Nick, Jason, Billy, and Arizonna were the only ones left. Ted Ginley tried to smile at me when he and his friends left. I just ignored him.

"Katie, didn't you see that?" Sabs whispered. "Ted looked like he wanted to talk to you!"

"Well, I definitely don't want to talk to him," I told her. "He was being a real jerk. I mean, he came with tons of people and started a fight with Scottie and everything. They're the ones who brought beer, too."

Randy shook her head. "What a bingo head."

"It's a good thing you found out what he's like before he asked you to go out with him again," Al added.

I certainly agreed with that. I never wanted to see Ted Ginley ever again in my life!

Sabs bent down and picked up a few empty cans that had been dropped on the carpet. "Could we stay and help clean up?" she asked one of the police officers.

The officer looked down at Sabs and smiled. "It's getting kind of late, young lady. Why don't you go on home now and come back tomorrow. Believe me, this mess will still be here in the morning."

Billy's oldest brother showed up just as the policemen were leaving. He was a little late to break up the party, but he was just in time to drive Billy and the guys home. Reed offered to take Sabs, Randy, and Al in his car.

After everyone had finally left, Michel, Emily, and I sat in the family room in silence.

"Em, I'm really sorry," I said softly, forcing myself to look at her.

"Me too. It was all my fault. Katie didn't even want to have a party," Michel confessed.

Emily wouldn't look at either of us. She just stared stonily ahead, with her mouth clamped shut and her arms crossed over her chest. It was the angriest I had ever seen her.

"Emily?" I prompted, feeling a little scared. "Say something!"

She finally turned to glare at me, and then at Michel. "I cannot believe you two did something so stupid. And to think that I trusted you!" Without another word, she got up from the couch and stormed upstairs.

Michel and I just looked at each other. I was feeling really awful, and I could tell he was, too. Finally he stood up and said, "So I guess we better get cleaning, eh?"

Michel sat down on the carpet and began to gather the CDs and VCR tapes and alphabetize them, the way Jean-Paul had left them.

I decided that the first thing I needed to do was look around downstairs and see exactly how terrible the damage was. I started with the kitchen, which was a complete mess. Food and soda were spilled everywhere, and there were lots of broken glasses and beer bottles.

The foyer was almost as bad. Mud had been tramped across the wooden floor — it would definitely have to be mopped. Luckily, the parlor was okay, except for the cans and bottles that were scattered around on the floor. It seemed like people had mostly kept to the family room and kitchen.

I stopped short when I went into our dining room. The glass door to our china cabinet was wide open, and one of the plates had fallen to the floor and cracked in two! I picked up the two halves of the blue-and-white plate and looked at them in horror. I knew these plates had belonged to Jean-Paul's grandmother, and now one was broken!

Running back into the family room, I held the two halves up so Michel could see.

"Oh, no!" he gasped. "How did that happen?" I could tell he felt just as bad as I did.

"It's my fault, too, you know," Emily's voice said behind us, surprising me.

When I turned around, I saw that she was standing in the doorway. She didn't look angry anymore, just upset.

"What you did was wrong," Emily went on in a quiet voice. "But I'm the one that was selfish and went out to a party and left you two alone when I knew Mom wouldn't approve. You guys were my responsibility. Mom and Jean-Paul trusted me, and I failed."

She was being really hard on herself. "Don't

feel bad, Em. We were all wrong," I told her.

"So what do we do now? Do we confess to Mom and Dad?" Michel asked. I could tell by the look on his face that telling about the party was the last thing he wanted to do.

"I don't know if I can lie anymore to Mom and Jean-Paul," I told him. "I feel guilty enough already."

Emily pointed to the broken plate. "Besides, once they see this, we'll have to tell them," she said.

She looked slowly around the family room. "But maybe if we get everything cleaned up really well, they won't be so mad about the party," she suggested.

That was the best idea I had heard all night. We began with the pool table. I had never realized it was so heavy until we tried to turn it back right side up! It took all three of us a long time and lots of muscle to get it standing again.

Michel ran his fingers carefully over the felt. "Whew! The felt is fine, and I don't think the slate top is cracked," he reported.

That was a relief. Now we just had a million other things to worry about.

I tried to remember what time Mom had

said she would be home tomorrow. Late afternoon, I was pretty sure. We would definitely need every minute until then to clean up this mess!

We cleaned for about an hour until the three of us were so exhausted that we were about to drop.

"How about we finish this in the morning?" Emily suggested, tiredly brushing her hair out of her face. The room was a lot neater, but it still definitely looked like there had been a party there.

"*Oui*," Michel said, yawning. "I think that is a good idea."

I hesitated. I really wanted to get the cleaning done, but I felt too tired to even move. "Okay," I finally agreed. "Anyway, Sabs said she'd come over to help with Randy and Allison."

I felt like a zombie as I dragged myself up the two flights to my room, changed into my nightgown, and brushed my teeth. I don't think I had ever been so happy to crawl into bed. The minute my head hit the pillow, I fell sound asleep.

Chapter Eleven

The next thing I knew, it was daylight and the phone was ringing. I grabbed the receiver and said in a sleepy voice, "Hello?"

"Katie! Are you still in bed?" Sabs's voice yelled into my ear. "It's eleven-thirty! Don't you have to have the house clean by four?"

My eyes flew open, and I looked at my clock. Sabs was right — I had to get moving! "Oh, no! Sabs, I have to wake Michel and Emily. Can you guys come over right away and help?" I cried in a panic.

"Sure, that's what I was calling about. We'll be over in half an hour," Sabs assured me. "And this time, I promise, we won't be late!"

"Thanks. Bye!" I quickly hung up the phone and jumped out of bed.

I ran through the bathroom to the connecting door to Michel's room. "Wake up, Michel!" I yelled, pounding on the door. "It's late!"

I didn't even wait for an answer. Running back into my room, I just threw on the same jeans and sweatshirt I had worn the day before. Then I hurried upstairs to Emily's room. As soon as I was sure she was awake, I ran down to the first floor.

Things looked just as bad in the daytime, if not worse than they had the night before. The family room carpet was still full of ground-in food, and the foyer hadn't been cleaned at all!

The first thing I did was get a mop and start cleaning up the mud in the foyer. Emily and Michel both came downstairs within a few minutes. Michel got out the vacuum cleaner and tried to get all the potato chip crumbs out of the thick carpet in the family room. Emily went to work in the kitchen.

We hadn't made very much progress when the doorbell rang half an hour later. I was really relieved when I opened the door and saw Sabs, Randy, and Allison standing there.

"You guys are just in time," Michel said, coming up behind me. "The inside of our house still looks like a disaster area!"

"The inside isn't the only part of the house that needs help," Randy said. "Have you looked out here lately?"

Michel and I stuck our heads outside to see what she was talking about.

"Oh, no!" I gasped at the same time as Michel said, "Mr. O'Reilly is going to kill us!"

The evergreen bushes next to the front door were all broken and mangled. Our gardener always kept all the bushes perfectly trimmed. He would notice this for sure!

"It must have happened when the guys hid there last night," I said.

"Don't worry, Katie," Al said, turning to me. "I think I can fix it."

"You can?" I asked.

Al nodded. "Sure, I help my dad trim our bushes all the time," she said, smiling at me. "Where are your hedge clippers?"

I figured we didn't have anything to lose. "They're in a shed behind the garage," I told Al, pointing her in the right direction.

Sabs wrinkled up her nose as the rest of us walked inside. "Katie, this whole house smells like beer!" she said.

"I don't smell anything," said Michel, sniffing the air.

"That's because you're used to it. I can smell

it, too," said Randy.

"Oh, no! What can we do?" I cried.

Sabs bit her lower lip, thinking. "We need some air freshener and some lemon cleaning stuff," she said. "That hides any smell. Believe me, we have a dog, so I know what I'm talking about!"

"I'll take care of it," Randy offered. "The cleaning stuff's in that room off the kitchen, right?"

She started down the hall, then stopped to look back at me. "So, Katie, I guess by this mad cleaning rush, you decided not to tell your parents?" she asked.

I shook my head. "No, we're going to tell. We just thought that if the house was neat, they might not be so mad about it."

"That makes sense," Sabs said as Randy disappeared into the kitchen. She looked around at the cans and bottles that were still in the parlor. "I'll clean up all of those," she offered. She got a big black garbage bag out of the pantry and went to work.

I didn't think we were ever going to get everything done. But when I looked up three hours later, the house looked perfectly clean and the bushes outside were trimmed and neat-looking.

The last step was to lug all the garbage bags over to the Acorn Falls Country Club bin so that our yard wouldn't look messy. We all trooped back inside just as Emily came out of the kitchen.

"I put a roast in the oven. It should be ready for dinner after Mom and Jean-Paul get home," she told us.

We all took one last look around the house. My stomach flip-flopped when I saw the broken plate on the dining room table. But at least everything else was neat and orderly.

"We did it!" Michel crowed. "And it is only three-thirty." Turning to Sabs, Al, and Randy, he said, "You guys saved us. Thanks."

I happened to look through the sheer white curtains covering the front window.

Just then a long black car was pulling into the driveway.

"Ohmygosh, here they are!" I cried. "They're early!"

"Relax. Everything is cleaned up," Emily said.

Then I remembered something. "Jean-Paul's

cognac!" I gasped, grabbing Michel's arm. "Did you put it back in the bar?"

His face turned completely white. *"Mon Dieu!* Where did I hide it last night?"

"Find it!" Emily told him, looking panicked.

I looked out the window again and saw that the driver was unloading Mom and Jean-Paul's luggage from the limo's trunk. They would be inside any second!

"We'll have to stall them!" Sabs cried.

Before I knew what was happening, she grabbed my arm and pulled me out the front door. I didn't know if I was ready to face Mom and Jean-Paul yet, but I didn't have a choice.

"Mom! Jean-Paul!" I exclaimed, running over to hug them. "Welcome home!"

Sabrina came right over and began asking a million questions about their trip and Bermuda and the weather. I didn't hear a word they said. I was too busy worrying about Michel finding Jean-Paul's prized bottle of cognac and putting it back where it belonged.

"Brr. It's chilly back here in Minnesota!" Mom said, beginning to walk toward the door. "I guess I got used to the warm Bermuda sunshine."

I jumped in front of her. "I'll get the door for you, Mom!" I cried.

I opened the door a little, blocking her view with my body. Michel ran across the foyer with the bottle of cognac. He grinned at me, then shot into the parlor to return the bottle to the bar.

Taking a deep breath, I pushed the door open all the way. Emily, Randy, and Allison were all standing expectantly in the foyer with big smiles on their faces. Michel ran out of the parlor and joined them just as Mom and Jean-Paul got to the doorway.

"Welcome home!" they all cried.

Mom looked really touched that we were all so happy to see her. "How sweet!" she exclaimed. "And what have you children been up to while we were gone?" she asked.

Sabs looked from Randy to Allison. "Well, we have to go now," she said. They quickly said good-bye and left us alone with Mom and Jean-Paul.

I took a deep breath. I knew it was time to confess. I was definitely dreading it, but at least Emily, Michel, and I would face the music together.

Don't miss
GIRL TALK #24
COUSINS

"So what's the big news?" Katie asked as we squeezed into a bright blue booth at Pauley's Pizza Parlor.

"Yeah,"Allison cut in. "You said this was really a big one."

"It is," I said. "Remember when I told you I had a cousin who lives in Paris?"

"You mean the one that's the model?" asked Allison.

"Right, that one," I replied.

"And she has this really weird name, like Zoo-ey or something?" prompted Katie.

"Zoe," said Randy. "Rhymes with Bowie. Like David Bowie. I love that name. It's so cool. If I ever have a daughter, I'm going to keep my last name and call her Zoe."

"Zoo-ey Zak!" Katie exclaimed. "Are you kidding?"

"ZOH-ee," Randy corrected again. "Why not? It's different. Zoe Zak. Cool!" She smiled to herself. "So what's the story, Sabs?"

"Well," I began, "Zoe's dad owns a few art

galleries, right? He's decided to open a few in the U.S. The first one will be in Minneapolis. So that's where they're moving!"

"Neat," Allison said as the waitress brought our sodas.

"But that's not the best part," I continued, taking a sip of diet cola. "Zoe's parents have to stay in Paris to finish up some business, so she's going to live with us for a couple of weeks!" I announced. "Isn't that awesome!"

"You mean she'll be going to school with us and everything?" asked Katie.

"Yeah! Since she's twelve, too, she'll even be in our classes. I think it's so cool: I can just see it now" — I paused dramatically, then raised my hand in a sweeping gesture like I was reading a headline — "'Sabrina Wells and Her International Cousin Take Bradley Junior High School by Storm!'" I sighed. "It'll be the biggest thing that's happened all year!"

TALK BACK!
TELL US WHAT YOU THINK ABOUT
GIRL TALK BOOKS

Name _____

Address _____

City _____ State _____ Zip_____

Birthday _____ Mo._____ Year _____

Telephone Number (____)_____

1) Did you like this GIRL TALK book?

Check one: YES_____ NO_____

2) Would you buy another Girl Talk book?

Check one: YES_____ NO_____

If you like GIRL TALK books, please answer questions 3–5;
otherwise, go directly to question 6.

3) What do you like most about GIRL TALK books?

Check one: Characters_____ Situations_____
Telephone Talk_____ Other_____

4) Who is your favorite GIRL TALK character?

Check one: Sabrina_____ Katie_____   Randy_____
Allison_____   Stacy_____ Other (give name) _____

5) Who is your *least* favorite character?

_____

6) Where did you buy this GIRL TALK book?

Check one: Bookstore____Toy store____Discount store____
Grocery store____Supermarket____Other (give name)_____

Please turn over to continue survey.

7) How many GIRL TALK books have you read?
Check one: 0_____ 1 to 2_____ 3 to 4 _____ 5 or more_____

8) In what type of store would you look for GIRL TALK books?
Bookstore_____Toy store_____Discount store_____
Grocery Store___Supermarket___Other (give name)_____

9) Which type of store would you visit most often if you wanted to buy a GIRL TALK book?
Check *only* one: Bookstore_____Toy store_____
Discount store_____Grocery store_____Supermarket___
Other (give name)_____

10) How many books do you read in a month?
Check one: 0_____ 1 to 2_____ 3 to 4 _____ 5 or more_____

11) Do you read any of these books?
Check those you have read:
The Baby-sitters Club_____Nancy Drew_____
Pen Pals_____ Sweet Valley High_____
Sweet Valley Twins_____Gymnasts_____

12) Where do you shop most often to buy these books?
Check one: Bookstore_____Toy store_____
Discount store_____Grocery store_____Supermarket___
Other (give name)_____

13) What other kinds of books do you read most often?
_____

14) What would you like to read more about in GIRL TALK?
_____
_____

Send completed form to :
GIRL TALK Survey, Western Publishing Company, Inc.
1220 Mound Avenue, Mail Station #85
Racine, Wisconsin 53404

**LOOK FOR THE AWESOME GIRL TALK BOOKS
IN A STORE NEAR YOU!**

MORE GIRL TALK TITLES TO LOOK FOR

Nonfiction

ASK ALLIE 101 answers to your questions about boys, friends, family, and school!

YOUR PERSONALITY QUIZ Fun, easy quizzes to help you discover the real you!

BOYTALK: HOW TO TALK TO YOUR FAVORITE GUY